The Boy in the Bubble

The Boy in the Bubble

Ian Strachan

First published in Great Britain 1993
by Methuen Children's Books Ltd
Published 1994 by Mammoth
an imprint of Reed International Books Ltd
Michelin House, 81 Fulham Road, London SW3 6RB
and Auckland, Melbourne, Singapore and Toronto

Reprinted 1994 (four times), 1995, 1996

Copyright © 1993 Ian Strachan

The right of Ian Strachan to be identified as author of this
work has been asserted by him in accordance with
the Copyright, Designs and Patents Act 1988

ISBN 0 7497 1685 1

A CIP catalogue record for this title
is available from the British Library

Printed in Great Britain by
BPC Paperbacks Ltd

Contents

1

How was I supposed to know it was going to be the kind of
day when you might get hit by a shooting star, or find an
extra strip of gum in the pack?

Until the end of school it had been full of the usual sort
of stuff. A new spot on my chin, a B– for English and Mel,
supposedly my best friend, giving me a black eye during
netball. We were supposed to be on the same side too!

Melissa not only has naturally wavy, thick, black hair
and a honey-coloured complexion but, when breasts were
handed out, I swear Mel went round twice and got my
helping too.

Currently, I am, as they say, mammarily challenged.

Put simply, I came out like an anorexic ironing board –
totally flat, spindly legs and with a white cover. If I
sunbathe, which is not often because I'm the unlucky kind
of blonde who burns and never tans, but if I do, it looks as if
somebody laid out a bikini to dry on a plain white towel.

Something resembling breasts by my next birthday, my
sixteenth, is my big ambition. Right now, I'd willingly
settle for shapely thighs, or even hips that don't stick out
like corner shelves.

So it was just my luck, that day, to come into contact
with the only part of Mel's body which isn't soft, padded
and round, her elbow.

The argument over the black eye was only one of the
reasons we didn't walk home together. The other was her

heavy date with Justin, James or John. To be honest it's hard to keep track. Either way, I didn't want to play gooseberry looking like the loser of a prize-fight.

So I'd gone my own merry way; frightening babies and turning milk sour. But as I reached the corner of our road, I noticed a removal van parked in front of what used to be the Naylor's bungalow.

Two men, one young and rather dishy, were humping tea-chests up the path. On the front step, watching their every move, was an overweight woman wearing tight jeans and a worried expression. Her stringy, blonde hair looked like a partial survivor from *Attack of the Overheated Hair-styler*.

The houses on our estate aren't allowed fences, or hedges, round the gardens and on her back lawn, just in the shadow of a huge sycamore, stood a big, transparent, plastic box on wheels. Like a small, travelling greenhouse.

Being nosy, and knowing the woman was busy round the front, I crept across the grass to get a better look at this weird contraption. I expected plants, or pets, but lying full length in it, wearing only blue swimming trunks, was a boy!

Now, I've always read the warnings they print on plastic bags. I know, if you stick one over your head, unless there are holes punched in it, you suffocate.

But there were no holes in this plastic. So naturally I assumed he was dead. Besides, to support my theory, his skin was pale enough, whiter than mine.

I tried to work out what kind of people move into a new house and leave their dead child on the back lawn for all to see? Maybe distant relatives of the Addams Family?

But when I got closer I realised he wasn't dead, he was lying on his side reading a book.

But if he didn't need oxygen to stay alive, what was he? An alien from outer space? His thick, unkempt, brown hair didn't look like an alien's. In fact it looked rather nice, especially the way it curled gently round his pale, slender neck.

But I'd got too close. My shadow fell across his book.

Squatting on his haunches, he swung round. Then he started to bounce up and down, scratching his armpits with his hands like a monkey, and letting out screeches which, even through the tough plastic, were ear-splitting.

Suddenly he stopped bouncing and shrieking.

For a second he just stared at me and then it was as if his face was melting.

One side of his mouth slowly drooped. His dark eyes squinted, his tongue appeared to swell and a long skein of spittle oozed over his lower lip to hang, glistening in the sun, like a transparent spider on a thread.

It was when he began to moan, low, slow, deep, unearthly moans, that I turned and fled across the grass. I slipped on some damp leaves and almost fell, but I kept on running.

By the time I reached home I was in an advanced state of nervous shock. Mum wasn't back from work, so I did the only thing I could, I made a humungous peanut butter sandwich.

I tried to ring Mel but she hadn't returned from playing Scarlett O'Hara.

I turned on the TV and watched cartoons to try and blot out the hideous image of the slavering boy, but that didn't work. Tom was chasing Jerry and Scooby Doo was being frightened out of his teeth by hideous, ghoulish monsters.

Worse still, one of the dead sycamore leaves I'd slipped on was stuck to the sole of my shoe and it reminded me of a huge, rotting hand!

By the time Mum got home I was a gibbering wreck.

'Anne, what on earth's happened to you?'

'Oh, Mum, it was terrible,' I wailed. 'There was this awful boy . . .'

'He attacked you?'

'No, but he moaned a lot and dribbled at me.'

'So how did he give you a black eye?'

I'd forgotten all about the eye. 'Oh no. That was Mel.'

'Of course, I should have known,' Mum said, slipping her shoes off, 'what else are friends for?'

It took several attempts to unravel the two stories, but in the end Mum realised it wasn't Mel who'd upset me, but the boy.

'But if you came up on him unexpectedly,' she pointed out, 'maybe he was scared too. Heaven knows, even on your best days, you scare me, but with that black eye . . .'

'Mum! Be serious! He must be a head-case, but why do they put him out there in a box? Do you think they keep him in the garage at night?'

'Anne! You're letting your imagination run away with you.'

My mother knows exactly how seriously to take me. Just talking to her, got rid of most of the horror. She's always been good at taking away pain, whether it's hurt knees, or hurt feelings.

Mum and I live alone together. I never knew my dad, he left home soon after I was born.

Mum always promises me it wasn't the shock of seeing me. 'He went out, alone, to celebrate New Year's Eve and for all I know he's out there still, singing "Auld Lang Syne". I've never seen, or heard from him, since.'

Mum jokes about everything, but I really believe she doesn't miss him one bit, which is odd, because she swears I was no accident. So she must have loved him once.

The only hint of real explanation she ever gave me was, they quite simply outgrew each other.

This confuses me even more. I mean, when I outgrow my clothes, I get new ones, otherwise I'd be a nudist by now and frightening the entire universe to death with my naked, knife-like body!

The fact is, if Mum no longer needs a husband, or any other man, as long as she's happy, I can cope without a father.

She hasn't been out on a date during my entire lifetime and that isn't because she's not pretty.

Her pale grey eyes always have a wonderful dreamy look about them and if she could afford to go to the hairdresser's more often, her soft, brown hair could be really attractive. Far better than my Dayglo blonde; all my father ever gave me!

Mum's had plenty of offers but, very sweetly, turns them all down.

But then, Mum's whole attitude to life is a little weird.

'Now,' she said. 'What shall we have for tea?'

'Snake steaks,' I suggested and went off to my room to start my homework.

I bet in your house, you could ask for something normal like boiled eggs, or baked beans and get them, but not in ours. Either Mum doesn't listen or she forgets.

Even when *she* chooses, she often forgets what she's cooking. Once she decided on spaghetti bolognese. Halfway through making the meat sauce, she thought we were having a pie and ran up some pastry. What we ended up with was curry and rice, and two dozen pastry bunnies with raisin eyes!

She's mad! Once she went to the office in her slippers. Another time I searched the entire house for my clean panties. Eventually I found them, in the salad drawer of the fridge.

She just laughs it all off. The only thing she never jokes about is school work. She's convinced I should go to university.

'Remember what happened to me! A woman should be able to look after herself. Get all the qualifications you can before you get married. That way you'll never have to rely on a man to keep you.'

Fat chance! The nearest I'd got to a boyfriend was when Darren kissed me behind the bike shed, if you'll pardon the expression.

Although Darren had terminal acne and no neck to speak of, I thought, at last I've got lift-off before I become too chronologically gifted – old to you!

That was until he started fumbling with my blouse and accused me of being more flat-chested than he was!

I may not be Madonna, but every girl has her pride and I'd have told him what I thought of him, if he'd hung around long enough.

So I'll probably live at home for the rest of my life.

'No you won't!' is Mum's standard reply to my pessimistic view of life. 'I'm not having you cluttering up the house for ever.'

'You wouldn't throw me out on the streets?'

'If you aren't gone by the time I think you should be, I'll sell the house and move without telling you!'

It's a good thing I never believe a word she says.

I decided to try Mel again. This time she was back.

'Hello, who is this?'

We dropped into one of our standard routines. 'Anne.'

'Anne who?'

'Anne O'Rexia.'

'Hi. Do you know Jason has an elder brother with a sports car?'

'No, but if you hum it, I'll join in the chorus.'

'Dummy!'

'Only when you have your hand stuck up my back.'

'Rob's wonderful,' Mel drooled. 'Blue eyes, brown hair . . .'

'And twin exhausts?'

'You bet!' she purred.

'Mel, don't be disgusting! Anyway, what about poor Jason?'

'Anne, he's so young.'

'Your age,' I pointed out.

'Exactly! Anyway, Jason always stinks of glue from those model aeroplanes he makes.'

'So you're trading him in for an older model?'

'I think I prefer my men more mature.'

Mum breezed through the hall. 'I often wish I'd bought shares in the telephone company. That way I could look upon the hours you spend on the phone as an investment.'

'Listen, Mel,' I said, after Mum had gone. 'I saw something really weird this afternoon.'

'A mirror?'

'Thanks! Oh, and thanks again for the black eye!'

'You ought to wear an eye-patch. That could be really sexy. Like Margaret Lockwood in *The Wicked Lady*.'

Mel's crazy about old films which she watches on Saturday afternoons while she's dolling herself up for dates. She knows the names of stars, people who died before my mother was even born, and all the films they made.

'Knowing me I'd end up looking like Long John Silver. But shut up, I want to tell you about this boy.'

That did it. I had Mel's undivided attention. 'Boy? What boy?'

Mel believes she knows every boy within a hundred square miles of here. She can't remember a single French verb, but you name a boy and she'll reel off not only height, weight, colour of eyes and hair, but go on to list their favourite foods, pop stars, sports, and especially what kind of transport they own. She's so obsessed with cars, she writes me notes in her favourite secret code which is number plate speak, or PL8SPK. You know the kind of thing: ILL MEAT U 2NITE A TATE.

Mel's a walking data bank of anything in trousers. She

13

doesn't just know how much pocket money they get, but what their parents do for a living.

I fed her the latest information. 'He's moved into the bungalow on the corner of our road.'

'Where the brown-haired boy with earrings lived – whose parents owned the shoe shop? The one into Heavy Metal.'

'I never knew a shoe shop that was into Heavy Metal.'

Mel ignored me. 'He had a 500cc Honda.'

See what I mean? 'Yes, Mel, the Naylors.'

'Pete Naylor,' Mel said, flipping through her mental card index system. 'He was nice, but a bit old even for me.'

'If you don't stop interrupting I'll never finish this story.'

'Sorry.'

But I should have known better. The moment I told her all about the boy in the plastic cage and how he'd frightened me to death, Mel realised he wasn't even a possible. A greenhouse on wheels doesn't rate as transport!

She lost interest and changed the subject back to Jason's brother, Rob. I made an excuse that Mum was calling me and hung up.

Mum wasn't calling. She wasn't even in the kitchen and nothing was cooking. I knew exactly where she'd be, in the spare room, called that because Mum spends every spare minute in it, it's her studio.

Mum keeps us by doing this really boring office job and, for her, real life doesn't start until she gets home. Then she paints every moment she gets. Pictures that is. Painting is her real love. She has a fantastic feeling for colour and shape.

Once, when I was tiny, she took me down to the City Art Gallery and stood me in front of a picture of some really evil-looking trees with scrawny, grey bark like elephant's hide. Trees which you felt could uproot themselves, walk towards you, catch you in their leafless branches and suck the very life blood out of you!

14

They really scared me, the same kind of scared as when I first saw the witch in Walt Disney's *Snow White*.

Anyway, Mum picked me up and showed me her signature in the corner of the picture.

All I could think of to say was, 'You could be really famous.'

Mum laughed. 'Only if I cut off an ear and/or die.'

But people do buy her pictures. It's just that she can't paint enough to sell and keep us and the house.

Which makes me feel a *real* liability. Why should she have to spend her life doing something really boring all day, just for my sake? I'm sure, if it wasn't for me, she'd go and live in somebody's attic, or something, and paint non-stop, day and night.

It's my guilt about that which makes me help out so much around the house. Besides which, Mum's hopeless with housework. Every spare minute she gets, she paints and I don't blame her. Everything else fits in as best it can. So what if the neighbours think she's weird for vacuuming at midnight?

The smell of turpentine hit me the moment I opened the door. 'In my next life,' Mum always says, 'I want to be a sardine, because I love working in oils.'

'Mum, what *are* we having for tea?'

Her palette knife, loaded with purple, hung poised before the canvas. 'What, dear?'

'I said, what's for tea?'

She looked puzzled, as if I'd suggested walking on water. 'Haven't we had tea?'

'Not yet. Shall I get us something?'

'Would you mind, Anne? I've been working on this sunset for weeks and I've nearly got it.'

She lives in another world. I think she's lucky, sometimes I'm not too keen on this one.

When I walked into the kitchen the first thing I noticed

was the blackened leaf that I'd brought home on my shoe. To this day I don't know why I didn't throw it away, but I didn't. Instead I pressed it, dried it out and I've still got it – though now it's only a skeleton of its former self.

2

About a week after my first encounter with the Boy Frankenstein, our form teacher, Miss Weinstock, stood up in front of the class. 'I'd like you all to pay attention. I have a special announcement.'

It was close to four o'clock and she had her hands clasped in front of her, which usually means she's going to say something really earnest, but any distraction's better than none! 'Tomorrow I don't want you to come to school . . .'

'Great stuff!' That was Mike.

'I mean,' Miss Weinstock added, pushing her glasses back up on to the bridge of her nose with her forefinger and glaring at Mike, 'instead of coming here we're going to meet at . . .' she paused to check the address in her file, ' . . . 127 Sycamore Grove.'

My brain snapped out of neutral.

That was where the Naylors used to live, where I had seen the mad boy!

But Miss Weinstock was still talking. 'Adam is unable to attend school. So from time to time we're going to hold classes at his house.'

That struck me as being about as sensible as inviting Einstein to a chimps' tea party. How could those of us who wanted to, concentrate with him, Adam, or whatever his name was, leaping around in his cage?

He'd been bad enough when it was just me, how much worse could he be with thirty of us all staring at him?

'Usually he has a special tutor who visits him,' Miss

Weinstock said. 'I realise the situation is a little unusual, but I'm sure I can rely on you all to remember, we're guests in the Simmonds' house.'

Then it hit me. This was another of Miss Weinstock's social projects. She's very keen on Community Involvement and is always arranging things like visiting old folks.

Mostly we're supposed to just chat, run errands, or help them with odd jobs, like decorating or gardening. In return they give us information for our Bygone Projects. Some people come back with fantastic old sepia-coloured photographs they've been lent. I've never got anything yet.

The last lady I visited, who Miss Weinstock told me desperately needed company, wouldn't even open the door to me. Probably because she was slightly deaf she never realised why I was there.

'No, you can't have your ball back!' she kept shouting at me through the letter box.

I called six times, but with no success. I can't help wondering if she really needs company, but personally I'm getting desperate. After every visit, I'm the one who ends up feeling lonely.

I've got a lot of time for Miss Weinstock. At least she notices you're alive, which is more than can be said for some. In another teacher's class, Josie got a really bad nose bleed. She waved her arm around for ten minutes before that teacher noticed. By the time Josie finally got permission to go to the cloakroom she looked like a *Driller Killers'* victim!

But sometimes Miss Weinstock's weird enthusiasms get a bit overwhelming. She always goes on these Special Interest holidays. No harm in that, but when she comes back we're all expected to join in. One summer it was Aztec art; the next it was tapestry.

At this particular time we all knew she was going steady

with a social worker, which probably explained how she got involved so quickly with Adam.

Miss Weinstock was still talking, ' . . . so that's what Adam suffers from.'

I'd obviously missed the important bit. But then, I already knew, better than she did, exactly what his problem was. As the bell rang for the end of school I decided to have a quiet word with Miss Weinstock to see if she really understood what she was letting herself in for.

I caught up with her on the way to the Staff Room. 'I wanted to tell you, Miss Weinstock, I've already met Adam . . .'

'That's nice.'

'I wondered, do you realise he's . . .' My voice trailed away. Now it had come to the point, I couldn't decide how to phrase it.

Miss Weinstock stopped and turned the twin beams of her big-framed glasses on me. 'He's what?'

'Out of his tree!' I blurted out. 'Oh, I'm not surprised,' I burbled on, 'I mean, keeping him in a plastic rabbit hutch would make anyone a bit weird.'

'Anne!' Miss Weinstock frowned at me. Her voice was very quiet, but I could tell she was really angry. 'For a start I don't like to hear you talking about mental health problems in those terms. Secondly, I think you should know that Adam has a very high I.Q.'

'Perhaps there was a mix-up with the test papers,' I suggested helpfully.

'Anne, just be there at nine o'clock, all right? And try to leave your prejudices at home!'

And with that she swept off into the Staff Room, leaving me standing in the corridor. Which is all the thanks you get when you try to help people! I should have known better. All I'd wanted to do was warn her, but if she wasn't ready to listen that was okay by me.

· · ·

When I woke the next day, the first thing I heard was rain on the windows. I was quite relieved about that. At least we wouldn't have to sit around Adam's cage in the garden, where all the neighbours could see. Obviously they didn't keep him out there all the time. In fact, come to think of it, I hadn't seen him since that first day.

Mum was already dressed and ready for work when I walked into the kitchen. I felt as though I'd hardly slept all night and my head ached as if an elephant had sat on it.

'You look terrible,' she said with a smile.

'Thanks, I feel sick.' The whole thing about our first meeting was really starting to get to me. Maybe I was the one who drove him over the edge? Suppose he was perfectly all right until he caught sight of me and then started leaping up and down again?!

'If you're sick,' Mum suggested, 'maybe you should stay at home.'

I'd already toyed with that idea. It was very tempting, but, apart being a complete cop-out, I didn't want to miss seeing the expression on Miss Weinstock's face!

'I'll be all right if I take an aspirin.' I opened the box we use as a medicine cabinet, but found only a bottle of picture varnish, a rusty safety pin, three sheets of sandpaper and two plasters. 'Where are the aspirin?'

'Where they always are,' Mum said without looking up from her newspaper, 'in the cutlery drawer.'

'Silly of me to forget!' I took two tablets with some milk and felt slightly better.

Because we lived so close, I didn't have to set out as early as usual but, hanging around after Mum left, I began to have dreadful visions of what might happen at the boy's house.

The worst version was when the boy got really mad and ripped through the plastic sheeting, like Freddie Krueger ripping his way through the wall in *Nightmare on Elm Street*.

Well, Elm Street and Sycamore Grove aren't all that far apart, are they?

I'd almost changed my mind and decided to stay at home after all, but at two minutes to nine, when I'd managed to stop myself shaking, I grabbed my books and wobbled off up the road.

I could see the boy's home the moment I left mine but, although I kept walking, it didn't seem to get any closer. The faster my legs moved, the further the bungalow seemed to go in the opposite direction.

I've never been exactly thrilled with my cocktail stick legs. Once Mel and I bought some stretch jeans, but you couldn't tell I was wearing mine. It looked as if two black snakes had sloughed their skins. Mel's were so skin-tight, you'd think she'd need surgery to remove them.

Needless to say, by the time I arrived, everybody else was already inside. You would have thought Mel might have waited for me!

By the time I'd eventually made it to the Simmonds' doorstep, my courage failed completely but, as my finger fell back from the bell-push and I was about to do a runner, the front door was flung open.

Mrs Simmonds stood there, looking as surprised as I felt, holding two empty milk bottles, the curls in her blonde hair so tight they looked like spaghetti hoops. 'Not another one!' she groaned.

'No,' I said, before I could stop myself, 'I'm the Avon lady.'

'I'm not in the mood for silly jokes. Come in, if you're coming!' It was obvious she was a good deal less thrilled than Miss Weinstock about us all visiting the boy. 'And wipe your feet!' she snapped.

Living with my mother, I'm apt to forget how real people behave. I'm always surprised when I visit Mel's and they have ice-cream as the *last* course.

'I'm sorry,' I said, jumping back and dropping my books on her toe.

'They're through there,' she said waving me towards the sitting-room door, 'if you can get in.'

To be honest, by now, I'd expected them to be pouring out towards me, recoiling in horror from the crazed boy, but all I could hear through the door was Miss Weinstock's voice, which sounded perfectly normal.

'Are you going in?' Mrs Simmonds demanded. 'Or are you going to stand there blocking the hall all day?'

'I'm sorry,' I apologised for the second time.

I opened the door and the sight inside was a greater shock than anything I could have dreamed up.

Although it was a large room, my class were crammed in round the edges of it, because almost the whole space was filled with a huge version of the plastic tent in the garden.

This tent was divided into compartments and the boy was in the largest section. Far from all the things I'd imagined, he was sitting, wearing a tee-shirt and jeans, looking out at us through the transparent wall whilst doing nothing more alarming than sucking the end of his pen.

'Anne, good of you to find the time to join us,' Miss Weinstock said icily. 'Perhaps you'd care to find a space and sit down before you trip over your bottom jaw.' I shut my gaping mouth and started to go red. 'I believe you've already met Adam.'

'Yes,' I admitted, foolishly trying to explain what I'd previously said to her by adding, 'but he looks quite different fully clothed.'

Naturally the whole class fell apart and I went even redder, especially when I noticed Adam grinning too.

I sat down in the corner so quickly that I knocked an ornament off the coffee table. Now, if I *really* wanted to draw any more attention to myself, all I had to do was spontaneously combust, or levitate a little!

I don't remember much about that first lesson. I spent most of the time trying to recover from my embarrassment and the rest keeping a beady eye on Adam for signs of imminent mental collapse.

Of course, there were none.

He just sat in his monstrous, see-through Wendy house looking about as innocent as a new-born baby. He was sitting at a desk which was smothered with pens, paper, paints and drawing stuff. Behind him was a bright red, two-seater settee and some free-standing shelves crammed with books. In one of the other sections I could see a small chest of drawers and a bed with a brightly covered duvet.

I had to admit, when he wasn't doing his Quasimodo impression, he was quite good-looking. There was a slight wave in his thick, untidy, badly cut hair and his astonishingly brown eyes looked deep enough to swim in. He had finely drawn eyebrows, even, white teeth and lips that were . . .

Well, if you really want to know, I wanted to throw up. I was so sick at having made a total prat of myself in front of him and the entire class!

Whenever Miss Weinstock stopped talking, I noticed vague humming and hissing sounds, which I guessed must be some kind of life-support machine. There were some tubes round the far side, but they were attached to the bubble, not to Adam. He seemed free to move anywhere inside.

It wasn't until we were leaving, when he stood up too, that I realised he wore no shoes or socks. The floor was also plastic, through which I could see the carpet.

'Adam, we'll be back at the same time next week, if that's all right?' Miss Weinstock said.

'I'd like it, but you'd better warn my mother,' he said. It was the first time he'd spoken since I arrived. His voice was quite deep and I realised it was coming out of a speaker, which I guess made it easier to hear him through the walls and he must have been listening to Miss Weinstock the same way. Spooky really.

Miss Weinstock smiled. 'I'll mention it on our way out. Come on, everybody, next class is straight after break as usual. I know you'll miss break, but I'm sure you'll all agree it's been worthwhile coming here.'

Before anybody could answer. Adam chipped in. 'It certainly has for me. I was really glad of the company.'

Miss Weinstock beamed and Adam sounded a right goody-goody.

We were just filing out when he called out, 'Anne!' and beckoned me back.

Reluctantly, dreading a repeat performance of his monkey act, I took a step towards him.

'I'm really sorry I scared you the other day.'

It was nice of him to apologise, but he'd forgotten about the amplifier and that everybody in the room could hear him, including Miss Weinstock. It was about as private as having your vital statistics read out on a local radio station.

'Forget it!' I stammered.

Then he said, 'Why don't you come back after school?'

I swallowed hard. 'I'm not sure, I'll try.'

Mike blurted out, 'She'll only come if you promise to keep all your clothes on!' and everyone giggled as I pushed through them, to escape before Adam could say anything even more embarrassing.

'Get you!' Mel said as she caught up with me. 'You've got your first date.'

'Yes,' I said, going deepest red, 'in front of the whole class and with an oxygen tent!'

3

'What's your problem?' Mel kept asking me for the rest of the day.

'Oh, nothing,' I said airily. 'He's male and under pensionable age. In fact, I can't think why you're not after him.'

I couldn't help noticing that Adam was the first male to arrive new in the district who hadn't been subjected to what's known as Mel's Test Drive. This often took place before their parents even had time to connect up the cooker!

Afterwards, all their names were carefully filed away, together with their distinguishing characteristics, plus points for owning a Lamborghini and minuses for bad breath, or dandruff. Needless to say, in Mel's league table, a Porsche owner with halitosis still comes out ahead of a motorbike owner with immaculate fingernails.

Not that I want to give the impression that Mel is loose. On the contrary, tight is what she is! Once a boy gets on her list, no matter how far down the league table he appears, there's no escape. He's never struck off. Not unless he commits suicide or, in our opinion far worse, goes out with Debbie Summerfield. Neither of us can stand Debbie. Anyone who can *must* be bad news!

Of course, Mel doesn't actually go out with all the boys on the list – mainly because there aren't enough days in the year – but they stay in her pending file.

You'd think they'd get bored with having to wait for their

next turn. I would. Once I pined for a whole week over a boy called Jimmy, who not only had more conkers than I had, but more teeth too! It only took me a week to get bored and give up on him.

But boys hang around Mel like clothes on hangers, just waiting to be used. Sometimes they still plead for another date years after their Test Drive.

For example, Tony has left school, been to college and Mel's had nothing to do with him since she invited him to her fourth birthday party (in those far-off days I guess she was assessing the relative merits of pedal-cars against tricycles) but he still rings her up for dates.

Needless to say, anyone who rings up while she's out isn't told what Mel's doing, her parents lie for her! They say she's in the bath, washing her hair, or with her maths tutor. As if Mel would need a maths tutor! At twenty paces, Mel can assess any boy's earning potential (allowing for a projected rate of inflation) minus tax, plus promotion prospects, without the aid of a pocket calculator!

I suppose I'm not painting a very rosy picture of Mel and you might be wondering why she's my best friend. And, if I'm her best friend, what do her enemies say about her?

In fact *my* enemies call me Mel's Fall-out Friend, accusing me of hanging round, waiting to snap up her spares, the ones who get fed up with waiting in line.

But I think you've probably realised by now, such a boy has yet to be born!

So it was all the more surprising that Mel showed no interest in Adam.

Then Mel provided the answer. 'How,' she asked, 'can you rate a boy who lives in a plastic tent?'

I should have known! He could have been a combination of Tom Cruise and Einstein but, being both immobile and inaccessible, he still wouldn't rate on Mel's scale. Even so, I was amazed Mel was giving up so easily.

'He is quite attractive,' she admitted. 'So's a butterfly in a case, but it's not much fun when you can only touch the glass, not the specimen. I suppose you could use him for practice, until someone better turns up. At least he's a captive audience.'

'Mel! That's sick!'

'No, it isn't, just practical. While you polish up your technique, he gets the benefit of your company. Sounds like a fair exchange to me.'

'Mel, you know perfectly well that isn't why I want to see him.'

'Isn't it?' Mel said, with an evil leer.

'No, I just feel sorry for him, stuck in there all the time. It's like the visits to the old ladies Miss Weinstock arranges.'

'Is it?' Mel smiled. 'Well, you could have fooled me!'

After all that, there was nothing else to do but ignore Adam's invitation. For a start, I resented Mel's suggestion that my technique needed polishing, even knowing it was true.

Sometimes Mel treats me like a kid. Anyone would think she wrote the original sex manual. I know all the theory, but I suppose that wouldn't stop me crash-landing when faced with the real thing.

But that had nothing to do with Adam.

So I walked home on the opposite side of the road, just to demonstrate that I'd made my mind up, something I'm not normally good at. I once found a book in our school library called *Making Positive Decisions* but couldn't decide whether to read it or not.

If Mel hadn't gone on at me, I might have called on Adam, now I knew he wasn't a weirdo. I did feel sorry for him, cooped up all alone, but in some ways I also found all that a bit hard to handle. I mean, how can you make friends with somebody in a plastic bag? It's like buying something really brilliant, but not being allowed to unwrap it.

Thinking through all this stuff had got me safely past the Simmonds' house, when a voice called after me, 'Excuse me!'

Mrs Simmonds was running across the grass, waving at me. Reluctantly I went back.

'You were with the lot that came to the house this morning, weren't you?'

Delighted about the unforgettable impression I'd obviously made, I nodded.

'Most of you left stuff behind,' she said, handing me a heavy supermarket carrier bag. 'I've spent all day clearing up after you.'

'I'm sorry.' I was at it again. Why did I keep apologising to this woman?

'As if I haven't got enough to do.'

'We'll be more careful next week.'

'Next week?' She sounded really gloomy at the prospect. 'I don't know if it's such a good idea. Adam has SCID. He's not used to hoards of people and he got really over-excited this morning.'

Before I could stop myself I said it again. 'I'm sorry.' But Mrs Simmonds, who seemed pretty overwrought herself, wasn't listening.

'When Miss Weinstock first suggested the idea, I wasn't keen, but she said it would help Adam. We've always managed before with just a tutor, but she went on and on and I was so busy with moving house – I just agreed. Now I'm not at all sure it's the best idea.'

'We'd all be very disappointed if we couldn't come,' I stammered.

For the first time she looked at me properly. 'Why?'

'Because . . .' my voice trailed away. I could hardly say, because I wanted to polish up my technique on him and it wasn't as if I fancied him.

Mrs Simmonds filled the gap for me. 'I suppose it's because you think he's some kind of freak?'

'Certainly not!'

'Oh, why then?'

I frantically groped around for an answer, any answer. 'Because it must be good for him to have company of his own age.'

Mrs Simmonds hadn't taken her hawk's eyes off me. 'Hmm. Well, we'll see.'

When she turned and walked back towards the house, I followed her. 'Adam asked me to pop in after school. Perhaps I could see him now for a few minutes?'

'No, you can't,' she said and slammed the door.

The phone was ringing as I walked through the door and I snatched it up. 'Hello?'

It was Mel. 'Who's that?'

'Anne.'

'Anne who?'

'Anne Oyed.'

She dropped the routine. 'Why?'

'Because Mrs Simmonds said I couldn't talk to Adam.'

Even over the phone, Mel couldn't hide the smug smile of triumph in her voice. 'I thought you weren't intending to go near him?'

'I wasn't, but on the way past their house his mother stopped me.'

'Why, was he pining for you already?'

'Don't talk wet. She only wanted to give me the stuff people left behind this morning.'

'I didn't leave anything.'

'Only your brain! Look, I've got to go, I've got homework to do.'

'I *knew* you'd try to see him!' Mel said triumphantly.

'Are you still feeling ill?' Mum asked, when she came home and found me buried in a medical dictionary.

During my search I'd realised I had the symptoms for everything from scurvy to sciatica, but they weren't what I was looking for. 'I'm trying to look up SCID, but I can't find it.'

'You're more likely to find skids in a car manual,' she said, dumping shopping on the kitchen counter.

'No, Mum, it's an illness.'

'And you think you've got it?'

'No, but Adam, the new boy who's moved into the Naylors' house . . .'

'The one who scared you to death?'

'The same. His mother said he suffers from SCID.'

'I've never heard of it. What's he like, now you've been within screaming distance?'

I tried to avoid her eyes. 'He's okay.'

'Okay? As nice as that? Wow!'

'Mum!'

'Do I need to start saving for a wedding?'

'Mum! I've had enough of that from Mel, don't you start. And why are you in such a hurry to get rid of me?'

'Because I want to let your room to Omar Sharif.'

'He's much too old for you.'

She smiled. 'How true, but Robert Redford's already got a room.'

Next day, to leave time to visit the reference library before class, I arrived early at school. My most unfavourite librarian, Miss Finch, was on duty. Mrs Unwin always smiles and helps like crazy to track down the most obscure information. But Miss Finch 'tut-tuts' the whole time you're in there.

She hates people touching *her* books. She twitches if you dare to take one off the shelf and hovers, in case you don't put it back in exactly the right place. If you dare to try and take a book out, she looks as if you're stealing one of her babies and when you bring it back she examines every page with a microscope.

'Good morning, Miss Finch,' I said with my sweetest smile.

'Mmm!' she murmered through lips like two slices of fresh liver.

I scooted over to the science section. Unfortunately, being so early, I was the only person in and she followed me, pretending to sort books while she kept an eye on me. I bet she thought I'd come in for a peek at the sex education books. If only she knew what little use I had for those!

I looked up SCID in two medical dictionaries without success. Neither time, nor Miss Finch, were on my side and in my hurry the inevitable happened, I dropped one of her precious books.

It landed with a noise like a cannon shot. Miss Finch leapt forward to rescue her battered child.

'Really!' she said, stroking the cover with her hand, as if trying to calm it down after its ordeal. 'You people have no respect for other people's property! Are you actually looking for something special?'

'I want to look up the disease, or illness, know as SCID.'

'Why didn't you ask? You know we're here to help!' She pulled out the very book I'd been about to pick up.

'Thanks, but I haven't got time to read it now, may I take it with me?'

'I hope you'll look after it,' she said, handing over the book as if it were an injured canary. 'And next time, ask. I'd already found that information for Miss Weinstock. Why do you need it?'

'I think our dog's got it,' I lied and fled.

• • •

Miss Weinstock was already taking the register and I sat down just in time to answer my name. Which stopped them from doing the standing joke, begun by a previous teacher. Because I'm so thin, one day when I was off school, he asked, 'Is Anne really absent, or just standing sideways?' Feeble though it is, that one's stuck ever since.

I hate jokes about my figure, or lack of it.

Anyway, I'm not skinny, I'm three-dimensionally disadvantaged. Once, when I was little, to make myself bigger I wore three sets of clothing and stuffed socks under my sweater. Sadly, I'd chosen the hottest day of the year and apart from looking lumpy, I got hotter and hotter, but was determined not to give in.

In the end, I fainted. Passed right out on the floor. Of course people loosened my clothing, only to discover how much of it there was and immediately jumped to the conclusion I was planning to run away.

While Miss Weinstock started the lesson, I looked up SCID with the book on my lap, half under the desk, so she wouldn't spot me.

SCID or severe combined immunodeficiency: thought to spring from a genetic deficiency, probably caused by a mutant gene. The odds against it happening are probably greater than 10,000 to 1. Babies born with this problem have no natural resistance to bacteria, or any form of virus, so that the mildest infection can prove fatal.

In the past, many must have died soon after birth as a result of this condition but, now the problem has been identified, it is possible to sustain life, though in a very restricted environment. This has to be totally sterile, fed by oxygen, and everything which enters the environment must have been previously sterilised.

Though research continues into this condition, as

yet no solution has been found beyond the permanent confinement of the patient for their own protection.

Adam had to live in the plastic tent because he'd die if he ever came out. Not only that but, unless the scientists came up with some new discovery, he was doomed to spend the rest of his life stuck in there!

'Anne!' Miss Weinstock's voice made me jump. 'I don't think you've heard a word that's been said so far.'

Naturally I did the only thing possible and lied. 'Yes, I have, Miss Weinstock.'

'Then perhaps you'll astound us all by telling us what subject you've chosen for your term project.'

'Certainly. Severe combined immunodeficiency.'

While a few people, like Mike, who'd been educated at the Ronald McDonald School of Wit and Humour, muttered 'swallowed the dictionary?' remarks, Mel, knowing I'd finally flipped, gave me a pitying look.

Only Miss Weinstock showed no surprise, but why should she when she'd already borrowed the book I'd got? 'You mean the illness from which Adam Simmonds suffers. An extremely interesting idea, but very little is known about it. I don't see how you could do a whole project on it.'

I had to think fast. 'There's more than just the disease and its treatment. It's how the patient and those who care for him feel about living with little hope of him coming out. Not unless somebody comes up with a cure.'

'Well,' Miss Weinstock sounded doubtful, 'apart from the fact that Mrs Simmonds or Adam might not give you their permission, I think you've chosen a very tough subject. I only hope you'll be able to sustain it.'

So did I!

'You crafty devil!' Mel said, the moment we were outside.

'What do you mean?'

'I've heard of patients getting ideas about their nurses!'

'I'm not going to nurse him!'

Mel's voice was heavy with sarcasm. 'I bet you're not! But you've made certain of seeing plenty of him from now on, haven't you?'

'Anyway,' I said, trying to change the subject, 'what did you choose for your project?'

'Influences of the motor car on patterns of social behaviour.'

'Well, you've already done all the research on that. Will you include anything you've learnt in the front seat, or just the back?'

But, although I was trying to sound confident, I spent the rest of the day worrying about how I would ever be able to complete the project. Especially as the subject's mother wouldn't even let me into the house.

4

'Mum, have you ever got into something way above your head?'

'Often,' she replied. She was standing looking at the picture on her easel through half-closed eyes.

'What usually happened?'

'Naturally, I almost drowned, but I'm still here. What's this about?'

'During class, I was reading a book which explained all about Adam Simmonds' problem, SCID. Miss Weinstock noticed I wasn't listening and she leapt on me, demanding to know what subject I'd chosen for my term project. So, I said the first thing that entered my head.'

'SCID?'

'Yes.'

'Oh, dear. Sounds a rather difficult choice.'

'It wasn't a choice at all. I just blurted it out in front of the whole class and when Miss Weinstock offered me a get-out I didn't take it.'

'You could always say, now you've had time to think, you've changed your mind.'

'But I can't back out now,' I protested, remembering Mel's taunts and knowing how much worse they'd get if I chickened out. 'I've *got* to go through with it. The trouble is, to do that, I have to talk to Adam, but the last time I tried to see him, his mother behaved like a jailer and wouldn't let me into the house.'

'Well, if she won't let you see him, you could always write to him.'

'That's brilliant! No, hang on a minute! I bet Mrs Simmonds would have to open my letter to sterilise it, or something. If she took one look, she'd probably tear it up.'

'Surely not?'

'If only there was some way of getting straight to him, without having to go through her.'

'You could always break into the house,' she suggested.

I couldn't believe I was hearing right. 'What?'

But whatever she meant, Mum was already miles away, tilting her head to get a different view of her picture. 'Now I've managed to get the sunset right, I'm not sure what colour the river ought to be.'

I'd lost her completely. But I couldn't grumble. After all, I'd had her almost undivided attention for at least ten minutes. 'Try pink,' I suggested off the top of my head.

To my amazement, she agreed. 'Not a bad idea!' As I left, she was already mixing the colour on her palette.

I'll never be able to see things the way Mum sees them! Which is a pity, because she's got this brilliant filter she inserts between herself and the real world. It works like the ones you put on a water tap to filter out all the chemicals you don't want.

Mum doesn't just use her filter for painting, but for life too.

I remember once, when she couldn't get a sitter, she took me with her to the office and gave me some paper and crayons to play with while she was typing. Her fingers fairly flew over the keys, but when I looked up, her eyes had the same dream-like look they have when she's cooking.

It isn't a blank look. Far from it. It's brighter, far more alert than either typing, or cooking justify.

Anyway, this time in the office, I crept up behind her. She was copy-typing the technical details of a new building. Lots of very complicated figures. One mistake and she could have had them building another leaning tower of Pisa!

But she was doing it all perfectly, without a single mistake, until I suddenly asked her what she'd just typed. Then the keys all jammed and she came to a juddering halt. 'Anne, don't do that!'

'You've no idea what you're typing, have you?'

'Certainly not!' she said, as she untangled the metal letters which had meshed together tighter than a zip fastener. 'While I'm here, I work on automatic pilot. That way I can use my brain for other things.'

I wish I could do that, but I always end up daydreaming.

In search of comfort I rang Mel.

'Hello?'

'Hi, Mel, this is Anne.'

'Anne who?'

'Anne Gory.'

'What's your problem?'

'What makes you think I've got a problem?'

'That's usually when you ring me.'

I gave in. 'Mrs Simmonds won't let me see Adam. If I write to him, she'll probably stop him getting the letter. So, how can I get through to him, so that I can do my project?'

'Hang a poster round your neck?'

'Thanks a bunch!'

But in the end, what Mel said was right! That was more or less what I did.

Next time we had a class visit, I made sure I was first to arrive. I took my letter and sellotaped it to Adam's transparent wall. That way, only he could read it.

When he first saw me, I think he was a bit cross that I'd let a whole week pass without visiting him, but just the same, he hauled himself up off the settee and read my letter.

Dear Adam,

I'm sorry I haven't visited you, but last time I tried your mother said you were too tired and she wouldn't let me in.

The thing is, I've chosen SCID for my term project and obviously I can't do it without your help, because the most important part is how you feel about everything. There are so many things I need to ask.

I'll understand if you'd rather not get involved, but I really would like to do it.

Anne.

Adam had barely finished reading, when the others started to arrive. I made sure I sat well away from him and at the end of the session, I got out first. Whatever his answer was, I didn't want him shouting it out again, like a station announcer over his loudspeaker, in front of the entire class. Especially not in front of Miss Weinstock or Mel!

This was very smart, except of course it meant I'd condemned myself to having to survive the agonies of waiting for his answer for another whole week, until our next class visit!

That evening, I was in my room doing homework, when my extension phone rang. Thinking it was only Mel trying to annoy me again, I didn't exactly rush to answer. 'Hi,' I said.

'Hi, is that Anne?' asked a male voice.

I perked up a bit but, suspecting it was probably only one of Mel's cast-offs doing a wind-up I replied, 'Anne Tagonist speaking, who is this?'

'Well, Miss Tagonist, thanks for the wall-chart,'

'Who is this?' It couldn't be! 'Adam?'

'How many people's walls have you been sticking letters on?'

His voice, coming over the telephone right into my ear,

instead of through the tinny loudspeaker, sounded strange, even deeper.

'Are you still there?' he asked.

'Only just,' I mumbled.

'Sorry? I can't hear you.'

I struggled to pull myself together, but ended up talking gibberish. 'I didn't realise you were allowed out to the phone.'

'You must be joking!'

'Well, how . . . .?'

'I've got a phone in with me. I got it for emergencies. Mum panics in case there's a power failure, or something, while she's out shopping and my life-support system switches off.'

'I hadn't thought of that.'

'Nor had she, until a flash of lightning zapped the power supply to our old house.'

'What happened?'

'I started to turn blue and began to cough a lot. Most people call it suffocating.'

'Idiot! I meant what did your mum do?'

'Rang the emergency services and got instant delivery of a generator.'

'Well, at least that can't happen again.'

'No, but if I was alone in the house, I couldn't exactly hack my way out, run round the back of the house, start up the generator and then climb back in again! So my mum grudgingly allowed me a portable phone and my very own credit card.'

'What's that for?'

'To pay with, what else? You'd be surprised how reluctant people are to do things for you, especially in a hurry, without getting paid. "Help me, I'm dying." "Oh, a terminal case, will that be cash?" I can't exactly open a door and hand over the money, can I?'

'Adam, there are so many things I need to know, if I'm to do this project properly.'

'You're sure you want to bother?'

'Oh, yes.'

'I don't know that it's such a good idea. SCID seems pretty boring to me, but I suppose that's because I'm the one who's stuck with it. Personally, I'd rather talk about life out there.'

'I don't understand.'

'Well, what does wind and rain, blowing in your face, feel like? What does a sausage taste like? What does other people's skin feel like? The only skin I've ever touched is my own.'

'That's awful.'

'I've never experienced anything else, so it doesn't seem so bad. Just like you're used to being out there. But that's why, to me, it seems a waste of time to be talking about being a prisoner when we could discuss freedom. I've never had many friends of my own age and the people who do come, don't really *talk* to me much. Most people, even relatives, are too embarrassed to speak to me directly. They ask things like, "Can he read and write?", but they usually end up gawping at me, like a fish in a tank and nobody ever wonders how the goldfish feels about that. Of course, the doctors at the hospital ask questions all the time, but we never have proper conversations, and Mum's always too busy. Besides she's always trying to protect me. It upsets her if I want to talk about anything she thinks I'm missing out on, say like what I just asked about being in wind and rain.'

'All right. Maybe we could do a deal. I'll answer your questions, if you help me with my project.'

'Okay, that sounds fair.'

'But that isn't going to be easy, if your mum won't even let me through the door. I don't want to do the whole thing over the phone.'

'Don't worry. Mum can be a bit of a dragon at times. She's got a lot to cope with, looking after me and she's right, I do get tired when I get worked up. Which I did the first time your whole class came round. So choose a different day and I'll tell her I'm expecting you. She never likes disappointing me, so she'll let you in next time. I'd better go now. See you soon, maybe?'

'Can I come round tomorrow, straight after school?'

'If you're sure I haven't put you off.'

'I'm sure.'

'See you tomorrow then, 'bye.'

''Bye,' I said, casually.

But why, I asked myself, if I didn't fancy him, was I still holding on to the receiver, listening to the loving purr of the line he'd used, long after he'd rung off.

5

In spite of what Adam had said, when I turned up after school the following afternoon, Mrs Simmonds still welcomed me as warmly as if I'd been Godzilla's love-child. 'I suppose you'd better come in,' she snapped.

'If it's not a good time . . .'

She folded her arms across her chest. 'What's that got to do with anything? You went behind my back to get to Adam, so now he decides what's convenient.'

'I didn't mean to.'

'Really?' The painfully thin lines of her plucked eyebrows strained upwards in disbelief before she turned away and headed for the kitchen. 'Well, I can't stand around talking, I've got things to do. Anyway, you don't need me to show you where to find him.'

I didn't, but this time, visiting Adam on my own, felt very different.

The moment I opened the door, because the rest of the class weren't there, the room appeared to have expanded. The short length of light brown carpet between the lounge door and Adam's cabin, suddenly seemed to stretch out in front of me like a life-sized relief map of the entire Sahara desert.

Adam seemed strange too. It wasn't just that he'd tried to untangle his hair, but he seemed all hyped-up, which scared me slightly. What on earth was he expecting?

So when he said, 'Hi,' and this humungous, black snake struck out at me, I nearly shed *my* own skin!

Having scraped myself up off the floor, I realised I was the victim of nothing more dangerous than one of the long-sleeved, black rubber gloves, which usually hung down inside Adam's bubble from two port-holes. I hadn't realised they could be pushed through either side of the wall.

'Aren't you going to shake hands?' he asked innocently.

'Oh, sure,' I said, feeling stupid shaking a gloved hand. The rubber somehow dehumanised Adam's hand, making it feel rather spooky and very clinical.

I didn't feel much better when Adam added the information, 'These were the gloves Mum had to use to change my nappies when I was a baby.'

I've always felt queasy about medical stuff. I know people who can sit in front of the TV, eating blood-rare steak, watching surgeons perform real operations, but not me. Just the sight of a hypodermic syringe, even in a play when I know they're only pretending, has me diving for the off-button. If an ordinary rubber glove made me feel this way, had I really chosen the right subject for my project?!

But, for Adam, this was everyday stuff and he didn't notice my squeamishness. 'Sit down.'

I collapsed on to the first chair I came to.

'If you came a bit closer,' he suggested, 'we wouldn't have to shout to be able to hear each other.'

'Okay.' Feeling like a prison visitor, as I dragged across an upright chair, I remembered the head jailer. 'I don't think your mother's very happy about my coming.'

Adam grinned. 'She'll get used to it.'

'Or she'll stop me visiting altogether.'

'She won't do that. She might try to put you off, but she won't stop you.'

'I don't want to cause trouble.'

'You have to stand up for yourself.'

'I hate rows.'

'There won't be a row!' The edginess in his voice, through the loudspeaker, was sharp enough to cut me.

'And I don't like bad atmospheres either!'

'There won't be one,' he snapped.

'I can feel one now.'

'Only because you keep droning on and on about it.'

I stood up. 'Maybe I should go.'

'No,' he said anxiously. 'Please don't. I promise everything'll be all right. Mum's very over-protective.'

We lapsed into an uncomfortable silence. Then a thought struck me. 'Why do you always talk about your mother, never your father?'

Adam avoided my eyes. 'Dad's not around that much. Too busy working all the hours God sends to pay for the hundreds of extras I need.' Suddenly he lunged into a violent change of subject. 'Did you know that Adolf Hitler was a vegetarian?'

'No, but I don't think that makes him seem any cuddlier.'

'Or that he wasn't really a house-painter?'

'I've never given it a great deal of thought,' I confessed.

'That was all propaganda. Young Adolf was a real artist and he wanted to study at the Academy of Arts in Vienna, only they turned him down, twice. So he painted little pictures of houses on postcards to earn himself a living. That's where the story came from.'

'My mum's a painter,' I said, but he wasn't listening.

'Just think, World War II might never have happened if Hitler had been accepted for the Academy. Instead of wanting to rule the world, Hitler might have just gone round quietly painting it. I collect unusual facts, and jokes. Would you like to hear a joke?'

'Not particularly.'

'Why couldn't the skeleton go to the ball?'

'I don't know,' I groaned.

'Because he had no body to go with!'

After that little gem, another uneasy silence fell over us which Adam eventually broke. 'So, where do we start on this project of yours?'

'I'm not sure,' I admitted. Knowing I was coming, I'd been worrying about that all day. The subject was so enormous I still hadn't worked out where best to begin.

'Well, I've given it quite a bit of thought,' Adam said rather smugly. 'Apart from me and my medical background, you'll need to talk to my mother and get the whole thing into some kind of broader perspective.'

The pompous language he used, to prove he'd come up with clearer ideas than mine, made me feel my whole project was being hijacked. I suppose it also showed that because he was so shut off from the outside world, I'd tended to think of him as being some kind of educationally sub-normal cabbage. So it came as quite a shock to realise how little I knew about him and to realise how sharp his brain was.

But there was also something about the way he talked which flew straight up my nose. On the phone he'd been so nice and yet face to face he was quite . . . no 'quite' is not the word . . . *very* pushy.

Coldly I said, 'This *is* supposed to be my project.'

'Got any better ideas?'

Wishing I'd never had this one, I shook my head.

'Right, let's get started. I thought the first thing we should do . . .'

'We?'

'Well, you can hardly do it without me, can you?' He didn't bother to wait for a reply. 'We ought to draw a plan of my living space.'

Obstinately determined not to be bossed around, I clutched at the slightest excuse. 'I didn't bring anything to measure with.'

But Adam refused to be put off. 'That's okay, I've got a ruler, I can do the measuring. You draw the plan. It only needs to be a rough one for now, you can do it properly later.'

'I know!' The way he continually told me not only what to do, but *how* to do it, was really starting to get me.

I quickly sketched out the rough shape, divided it into sections and then wrote down the measurements as he called them out. Naturally, because Adam insisted on doing it in the most minute detail, down to the last millimetre, it took forever!

This is a copy of the finished version:

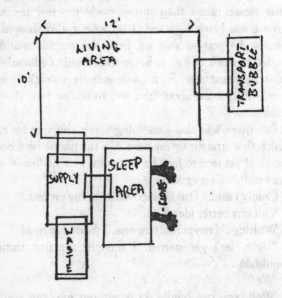

While I was still drawing, all kinds of questions came to mind. 'How does stuff get in and out to you?'

'Through the supply bubble,' Adam said, walking to the small section at the back. 'The whole process is a cross between leaving supplies on a stone outside a village during

46

the Plague and transferring stuff from a spaceship into a satellite. Everything has to be sterilised before it comes in here. My whole unit is made up of three compartments, each separated by air locks, so that they can be isolated. Although we're only inches apart, we never physically meet. I shut the air lock on my side, Mum opens hers, puts whatever it is in the supply bubble, reseals it and I have to wait until the air's been changed in the bubble before I can re-open it.'

'How do things get sterilised in the first place?'

'At the hospital. Everything has to go through them. Even after Mum's washed my clothes they go there to be made sterile and then they're packed in sterile bags and brought back. Not that my clothes ever really get dirty. I wash in sterile water and although I'm not allowed to use soap, that's not a problem because the air in here is filtered clean and temperature-controlled. That means I never sweat.'

'I can think of a few boys who could do with a deodorant like that!'

But Adam was concentrating on his lecture. Like a great many people who say they collect jokes, he rarely reacted to other people's. 'The hospital vets everything that comes in here. You'd be surprised what simple things cause problems. It was ages before they found a way to sterilise pencils and rubbers and although I've got water-colour paints, I'm still not allowed felt-tip pens.'

'And yet they managed to give you a phone.'

Adam shrugged. 'Like I said, they reckoned that could be a life-saver, so they went to a lot of trouble over it.'

'But the TV stays outside?'

'Yes, the innards would be difficult to sterilise, but it's partly for safety reasons, in case of fire. Fortunately they found one with all push-buttons so I can change channels by pushing them through the plastic sheeting. The plastic makes the pictures look a bit fuzzy. I use the gloves to change videos, but Mum won't let me keep the machine all the time because she says I watch too much. Trouble is, there isn't much that's physical to do in here, although I do have a set of exercises. But normally, when you lot aren't around, I don't get very tired and the video machine's useful when I have trouble sleeping.'

'What about food?'

Adam pointed to some low shelves, near the supply bubble, laden with tins. 'The hospital chooses that too.'

'But you haven't got a cooker, how do you heat things up?'

'I don't. Everything has to be opened and eaten at room temperature.'

As I scribbled down my notes, I couldn't help pulling a face at the thought of eating lukewarm ravioli or, worse still, macaroni cheese. 'Yuck!'

'I feel the same about warm food. Anyway, the tinned stuff is a big improvement on the little jars of baby food. I was on those for years, until they decided they could trust me with a tin-opener.'

'Why don't you have a microwave, then you could eat frozen foods?'

'I suggested that ages ago. They say it's not possible to be certain of getting the temperatures, or the cooking times, exactly right every time. So I couldn't be positive the food was totally bacteria-free. Oh, and before you ask, the crap goes out through the supply bubble too.'

'I wasn't going to ask!'

'Oh, most people wonder, but don't like to ask. I have to use this potty.' He shook a child's red plastic potty in my face. 'Degrading isn't it? But then, being totally dependent on other people for the smallest thing is pretty degrading.'

Adam started to prowl back and forth, reminding me of a hyena I saw in a zoo. The whole time I watched, the animal never stopped patrolling the cage's netting. But it didn't bother to stop and look for a way out, because it knew there wasn't one.

'It's the stupid things that get to me. Things you'd take care of yourself without even thinking. Before I was allowed to have anything sharp, like a knife, in case I punctured the plastic, my pencil sharpener broke once and I had to wait a fortnight to get it replaced.'

Wondering how you sterilised a plastic pencil sharpener, I nodded in agreement. 'That must be maddening.'

But Adam didn't seem to hear me. He was still pacing. 'It was about the same time that I tripped over, caught my arm on the edge of the desk and made it bleed.'

'Your mother must have had a job sorting that out using those glove things.'

He looked up, quite surprised I was still there. 'I don't remember that part. All I remember is how much it hurt and that all I really wanted was a hug, a proper one like all the people on TV have all the time.'

'But you do get out from time to time,' I said cheerfully, trying to change the mood. 'That's where I first saw you, remember?'

'Oh, yes! When I was in my transport bubble.'

'You really scared me that day.'

Adam grinned with pleasure. 'Really?'

'I told everyone a demented gorilla had moved in.'

'Maybe you were right. It's funny. You'd think that being stuck in here year in, year out, I'd be glad of any kind of escape but, you know, sometimes being out there amongst things I can see, but not touch, really scares me. Once, I was outside our old house, when a huge dog came and peed up against the wheel. I shouted at it, to try and get rid of it, but the dog began to bark and leap up to try to get me. The whole transporter shook and I was terrified the dog's claws would rip right through the plastic sheet. I've always known germs might get me, but that day I really believed I was going to die having my throat ripped out by a mad dog.'

'How terrifying.'

'I thought so. Funny thing was, when its owner came over to get it back, the dog looked quite small beside her. She said he only wanted to play. We mostly use the transport bubble for trips to the hospital. It fits straight into the ambulance.'

'Do you go there very often?'

'I used to, quite regularly, but now it's only for a couple of weeks a year.'

'Why do you go?'

'Always tests, and then more tests.'

'What for?'

'Search me, they seem endless. It's a miracle there's as much left of me as there is. I swear, over the years, they've taken enough skin, blood and stuff, to build another human being. Did you know there are bits of me all over the world?'

I swallowed hard at this ghoulish thought. 'How do you mean?'

'Samples of blood, skin, tissue and bone-marrow. They don't just take enough for themselves, they send bits to doctors all over the place to see if they can come up with some kind of an answer.' He added proudly, 'Last year they all gathered in Stuttgart to hold a conference just about me.'

'What happened?'

'Nothing, so far as I know. I don't think they're any closer to a solution now than when I was born. But I still go on giving. My blood and urine samples alone, if they'd all been preserved, would float your average garden-variety battleship.'

I was struggling hard not to throw up but, to Adam, this was everyday stuff. 'The only good thing about me going into hospital is, it means Mum gets some rest. She always says that's the only time she gets a proper night's sleep, when she knows I'm safe in the hospital with somebody else looking after me. It's tiredness which makes her so ratty.'

'Which reminds me,' I said glancing at my watch, 'I ought to go before I outstay my welcome.'

'There's no rush.'

'I think it would be better than waiting to be chucked out on my ear. Besides, I didn't tell my mum I was coming over here and she'll be wondering where I've got to.'

I'd already reached the door before he called after me.

'Anne, what kind of society do vampires join?'

'I don't know,' I said heavily.

'A blood group.' When I couldn't raise more than a sick grin he suddenly looked anxious. 'Everything's all right, isn't it? I mean, I haven't put you off, have I?'

'Of course not.'

His eyes, which looked like two shiny berries, scanned my face intently. 'When will you come again?'

'I'm not sure. I've got a million things on at the moment.'

'Make it soon,' he said.

'Of course I will,' I said, but I couldn't ignore a strange, surprising, niggling doubt which was already starting to form in the back of my mind.

6

I really intended to stick to my promise to Adam, about the visits and I did, up to a point. Of course some visits were more successful than others, but however well things went, hardly a time went by without me managing to put my bony, great foot in it. If not with Adam, then with his mother and sometimes both!

For instance, there was the blisteringly hot day when I raced round, clutching an ice-cold can of Coke I'd bought for him. At least it was canned, so I thought that would be okay. But when I arrived he gave me a pitying look. 'You can't sterilise Coke without killing the bubbles and wrecking the flavour.'

'Oh!' I said, disappointed that one of the first presents I'd brought him was something he couldn't have. Without thinking, forgetting I'd run all the way there, I jerked back the ring-pull and released a foaming jet of Coke which splashed all over Adam's wall, the living-room carpet and me.

Adam laughed himself silly, but when I went for a cloth to clean up the mess, Mrs Simmonds wasn't at all amused. Worse, instead of letting me clear it up, she insisted on doing it herself, while at the same time going on and on about it not mattering.

It seemed whatever I did when I was with Adam only helped to point out the huge difference in our lives and revealed less and less common ground.

Despite being winner of the Olympic gold medal for long-distance daydreaming, Mum quickly noticed things weren't going too well. 'I hope this Adam thing isn't going to get on top of you.'

'Why should it?'

'Oh, I don't know, guilt maybe.'

'Guilt?' I half laughed at her crazy suggestion. 'What have I got to feel guilty about?'

With Mum's usual knack of biting right through to the bone, she said, 'Because you're healthy, when Adam isn't and, perhaps most of all, because you've got your freedom.'

Although I'd already half considered the possibilities, naturally I instantly denied them. 'Oh, don't be silly. It's me – I keep saying the wrong things to him.'

But whatever I said to Mum, I was aware that the gaps between my visits *were* growing longer.

After one of the class sessions at Adam's house, Mel collared me. 'Have you and the wonder boy fallen out?'

'Of course not.'

'So why did you spend the whole of the last hour gazing at the carpet?'

'I didn't.'

'Yes, you did,' Mel said firmly. 'Adam, however, spent the whole time staring at you like a lovesick sheep.'

'You're making it all up.'

Mel grabbed my shoulders and made it difficult to avoid her eyes. 'You *do* realise he's in love with you, don't you?'

'You're mad!' I said, trying to break away from her.

'Anne, you'd have to be blind not to see! When you're in the room, he never takes his eyes off you. You do still see him outside class, don't you?'

'Oh, yes, but I've been a bit busy lately.' To slide away from the subject of Adam, I asked, 'How's your project going?'

To my surprise, it was Mel's turn to look uncomfortable.

'Not too well. I seem to have got a bit behind with my research.'

'I thought you spent every spare minute doing little else.'

Mel was wearing an expression I barely recognised on her face, guilt. 'Well, you remember I told you about Jason's elder brother?'

'Rob, the one with a Porsche 968?'

'The same. Well, I've spent the last few weeks with him.'

'Mel!' I said, trying to sound shocked. 'Surely you don't mean you've been going out with the same boy all this time?'

Mel nodded. 'Awful, isn't it?'

I couldn't help laughing. 'Mel, people tell me most girls only go out with one boy at a time.'

'But I've got my reputation to consider,' Mel protested. Mel's reputation was the kind most girls would rather not have, but obviously she didn't see it that way. 'Promise you won't tell anyone? I'm sure I'll get over him soon.' She made it sound as if she was hoping to recover from the flu!

'Mel, there really is nothing to be ashamed of,' I assured her, though she clearly wasn't convinced.

Searching for the smallest crumb of comfort from her usual condition, she tried to reassure herself. 'At least Rob doesn't know he's the only one.'

Her whole attitude baffled me. 'How do you manage that?'

'By staying in several nights a week, so he thinks I'm out with somebody else.'

'You're crazy! Why?'

Mel gave me a pitying look. 'Don't you know anything about men? If Rob ever found out he was the only man in my life, I'd lose all power over him.'

'Would it really be so terrible to admit that you're in love with him?'

'Then why won't you admit you're in love with Adam?'

'Because I'm not! That's why!'

Well, I couldn't be, could I? We kept falling out over the stupidest things. I never felt comfortable in his company. How could that be love?

And yet, at the same time, when I didn't go to see him, I missed him.

That night at dinner my mother said, 'Has my cooking finally got to you? You've hardly touched your food.'

I pushed my plate away. 'I'm really not hungry.'

'Then you *must* be sick. I've never known you eat less than a fatted calf a night ever since you were born.'

It's true. I used to say I was so thin because I've got tiny bones. If I had normal bones, I'd weigh as much as your average hippo. I eat tons of junk, bread, biscuits, cakes, crisps and chocolate. While other people swell up like force-fed pigs, all I get is zits.

Mum persisted. 'Are you sick?'

'If you must know, I'm worried about how things are going with Adam.'

She looked steadily at me. 'And how are things going?'

'Badly.'

'The subject proving too difficult?'

'If you mean SCID, no. If you mean Adam, yes.'

'You mean you don't get on?'

'It isn't that exactly.'

'You know, Anne, sometimes you aren't the easiest person to get to know.'

'That's not true!'

'You often hide yourself away, you always have. When you were tiny, if you fell over, you'd run into the house, trying desperately not to cry. Sometimes it took ages to find out exactly what had happened to you. As you've got older, it's your feelings you smuggle away.' Mum sighed and swept her hair back from her face. 'Maybe I'm partially to blame for that side of your nature.'

'I don't see how.'

'It's one of the problems of single-parent families. For years, having been the only grown-up around, I've got used to keeping my thoughts and feelings to myself. Besides, much of my emotional output goes into my paintings, which makes me more self-contained than most people. Sometimes, instead of sharing my thoughts with you, I go over and over them in my head, until I reach a point where I convince myself we've actually discussed them, or at least there's no longer any point in having the conversation. The trouble is, that way you don't get a chance to really have your say and it's only what *I* think you'd think!'

'Yes,' I admitted, 'I suppose I do that too.'

'Maybe, if you actually told Adam what you were thinking, shared it with him, that might make things easier.'

'I'll try, but it isn't easy talking to somebody who's shut away. Sometimes I feel as if I'm walking up to a shop window, trying to have a conversation with the dummy in the display. Not that Adam's a dummy, far from it.'

'Give it a try and remember, I won't pry but, if you need somebody to talk to, I'll always listen. Talking may not solve your problems, but at least it improves your appetite.'

I glanced down at my plate. I'd emptied it during our discussion.

7

When I finally turned up again at Adam's house, his greeting was hardly one, as Mel had suggested it might be, of undying affection. His crabby, 'So what brought you round here?' was hardly designed to smooth our path towards a newer, deeper relationship!

'I came as soon as I could,' I lied. 'I don't have all that much spare time.'

'I do,' he said blankly.

Two seconds into the room and I'd done it again. This wasn't working out any better than previous visits but, although my reaction was to want to walk out, I was determined not to leave without trying my mother's suggestion first.

'Look,' I said and took a deep breath, 'if you must know, the real reason I haven't been round is because I'm scared of you.'

Adam was so surprised, if he'd been a parrot he'd've slipped off his perch. 'Scared of me – why?'

'Because everything I say, or do, seems to get under your skin. No matter how hard I try, I always get it wrong.'

'No, you don't.'

'See what I mean? Look, I've got every sympathy . . .'

'I don't need anybody's sympathy,' Adam snapped back.

'Then what do you want?'

He turned away before simply answering, 'A friend. The trouble is everybody out there's too busy getting on with their own lives, even Mum. The rest, if they can be bothered with me at all, want to use me as some sort of emotional prop. Whatever Miss Weinstock says, I bet one reason why she brings you all here is because it makes her feel good. You've got to admit it, even you're using me, for your project.'

I flushed with a mixture of anger and guilt. 'But I didn't lie to you and we struck a bargain.'

'I've got a similar bargain with the doctors. I let them run any tests they like as long as they keep me going. Though sometimes I can't help wondering why they go to such enormous lengths to keep me alive.'

'But that's what doctors do! You know, all that stuff about the Hippocratic oath.'

'Sure!'

'You know they're trying to find a cure,' I insisted, 'so that one day you'll be able to come out of there.'

'I don't doubt it,' Adam agreed, 'that's what all the tests are about. I only hope they find the cure in time for me. Because if they can't, and I know this sounds selfish, I might as well rip my way through the plastic now and come out to join the living. And don't think I haven't thought about that, because I have, hundreds of times.'

'But you'd die within days, wouldn't you?'

'Probably, who knows? But, even if it was only for a month or so, at least I'd go knowing what it feels like to walk around in my own house, or to swim, or go up in an aeroplane. Next Wednesday I'll be sixteen. Sixteen years is a hell of a long time to live in ignorance in here, particularly if it's all been for nothing.'

A flash of inspiration struck me. 'Is it your birthday that's making you feel so sorry for yourself right now?' Then, the instant the words had left my mouth I wished I hadn't said them, but it was too late.

For a few seconds I thought Adam was about to explode. Angrily, he stalked away from me, but when he returned there was a lopsided, shamefaced grin on his face. 'I hadn't thought of it that way but I suppose you're right,' he admitted. 'Birthdays aren't just about opening presents, are they? They do make you think about your life and in my case, you must admit, there are some enormous, aching gaps. Take virginity.'

I gaped. 'What?'

'I may have SCID, but I don't have an arrested development. I've gone through puberty, just like everybody else. For me it's like being given a gun, complete with live ammunition, but being told you can't fire it under any circumstances. Safe Sex is the only kind I know about – I actually live in a giant condom!'

Although I knew he wasn't trying to be funny, I couldn't help laughing.

'Crazy, isn't it?' Adam persisted. 'I'm named after the first-ever man but, if it had been left to me, the human race would never have got under starter's orders!' Suddenly his smile faded. 'Anne, I'm scared of you too, you know.'

It was my turn to be surprised. 'Why?'

'Not just because you're the first girl of my own age I've ever really got to know, properly, but because I like you, a lot, and there isn't much I can do about that. I expect, when your project's finished, I'll probably never see you again.'

'Would you want to? I mean, we haven't been getting on a storm so far, have we?'

'That's mostly my fault.'

'No, it isn't,' I protested.

'Yes,' he said firmly. 'It's part of my whole thing of being too suspicious of other people's motives, but you've got to understand, stuck in here, I'm not able to chase people if they decide to walk out on me.'

I took a deep breath. 'Look, Adam, I'll be totally straight with you. I'll admit the whole project thing came about largely by accident and maybe, if it hadn't been for that, we'd probably never have got any closer than we do in class. But now, somehow it's different.'

He looked anxious again. 'So, when the project's over, you won't stop coming to see me?'

'I can't pretend all this is easy for me. All that heavy stuff about the future bothers me a lot and I'm not too certain how well I can handle it.'

'That goes for me too,' Adam said with a shrug.

'I can easily understand why you think about it so much, but it seems to me, "That way madness lies". Perhaps if we could just *be* from day to day. I don't mean ignore the truth, but maybe not dwell on it so much. To be honest, I have a big enough struggle coping with everyday living, without having it served up with a monster dash of Armageddon sauce.'

Adam nodded. 'I know what you mean.' Then he suddenly switched subjects. 'Do you have a boyfriend?'

What was I supposed to say – tell him his inexperience had led him straight into The Reject Shop or lie? Naturally, I lied, slightly. 'Not just at the moment.'

'Would you be *my* girlfriend?'

His eyes positively glowed at me. I swallowed hard. Until that moment, it was a question I'd only ever heard on TV, or read in books.

'Yes,' I said, casually, 'why not?'

'Me and nobody else.'

That was easy, the competition was not exactly beating a path to my door. I nodded.

Then he surprised me, by placing his hand upright, palm outwards, against the plastic sheet. 'Swear it?'

I put my hand up against Adam's. With only the thin sheet of plastic between us I was convinced that a massive charge of energy was flowing between us. A tremor ran through my body as surely as if he'd kissed me. 'I swear.'

• • •

The moment I got home I was on the phone to Mel.

'Who's this?'

'Anne.'

'Anne who?'

'Anne Gelus.'

'Oh, really? And who rang your chimes?'

'Mel, you were right about Adam.'

'Told you so. What happened?'

'He asked me to be his girlfriend.'

'Oh, so you're going out together?'

'More a case of staying in really, I suppose.'

'Yes,' Mel sympathised, 'hardly a question of holding hands in the back row of my cinema, is it?'

'Which is your cinema?'

'The Mel Odeon, where else?'

I suddenly yelled down the phone, 'Mel, that's a brilliant idea!'

Mel was rightly puzzled. 'It is?'

'Adam's sixteenth birthday is next Wednesday and he's always going on about things he's never been able to do. I bet he's never visited a cinema! So why don't I fix it as my birthday present to him?'

'Well, I'd say it's either that, or taking him to the Taj Mahal by moonlight. Are you crazy?'

'He could easily go in the transport bubble.' Then, amidst all the euphoria, a practical thought crossed my mind. 'I wonder if his air supply would last long enough?'

'Wonderful! I can just see the headlines: BOY CHOKES TO DEATH WATCHING *LOVE STORY*! Let's just hope it isn't a double bill.'

The cinema manager was no more enthusiastic when I went to see him at the local multiplex.

'My company does place enormous emphasis on access for the disabled,' he said, his voice oozing with the same kind of sincerity parents use before they add the unanswerable killer phrase: you'll understand why not when you're older.

'Then why not Adam?'

'There's the fire risk for a start.'

'It'd only be the same as having somebody come in a wheelchair.'

The manager shook his head. 'I wasn't thinking of him blocking the aisles. In purpose-built venues like ours that wouldn't be a problem. No, I was thinking more of the plastic cover and the air supply you described. I'm afraid we really couldn't cope with that. Besides, it can be very embarrassing for disadvantaged people, having people staring at them.'

'Adam doesn't look like an orang-utan, you know!'

The man, to his credit, held up his podgy hands in protest. 'I wasn't trying to suggest anything like that for a moment.'

But I was determined not to give up. 'Suppose there were no other people in the cinema at the time, then there'd be no risk to anyone but us, and nobody to get embarrassed.'

He smiled sympathetically. 'Fortunately, we don't have shows when nobody comes.'

I shook my head. 'I was thinking about hiring the cinema. People hire swimming pools for birthday parties, why not a cinema?'

He looked hard at me. 'Have you any idea how much that would cost?'

I shook my head and he named a figure that sounded like the year's national borrowing requirement! 'Ouch!'

There really didn't seem any way round all this and I was about to admit defeat, when he looked thoughtful. 'You say your friend's never visited a cinema before?'

'He's hardly been anywhere, apart from home and the hospital.'

'Do you think he'd mind a photograph appearing in the newspaper?'

'I don't understand.'

The manager leant across his desk. 'It would be a momento of his visit here.'

I was catching on. 'You mean, taking a picture of him to use as publicity for the cinema?'

He smiled, but quite genuinely. 'If you like, but I was really thinking of a way round the difficulties. You see, I have to account to head office for everything that goes on here.' He held up a thick sheaf of computer print-outs. 'Every ice-cream we sell, comparative indoor and outdoor temperatures, let alone who comes in. So you see, it would be impossible to get your friend in without permission from head office. That could take ages, which we don't have if his birthday's next Wednesday, and head office find it easier to say no to anything slightly unusual. But I've just thought, we hold previews each week.'

'Previews?'

'When we invite the press and local critics in to see new films, the ones which will be going on show the following week. Now, strictly speaking, those aren't public performances and I'm free to invite who I like. But, as the press will be here anyway, and just in case word got round, I could justify your friend being here if the cinema got some publicity out of his visit.'

'You mean, make an exhibit of him?'

The man had the grace to smile apologetically. 'I'm sorry, it's the best I can offer.'

8

'Absolutely not!' Mrs Simmonds said, the moment I broke the news of my brilliant idea. 'I've never heard of anything so ridiculous!'

It was a good thing I'd decided to approach her before mentioning my surprise to Adam. I'd even made certain of creeping round to the kitchen door, so that there was no chance he'd know I was there until I had Mrs Simmonds' blessing.

I'd only asked out of courtesy, the idea that she'd refuse had never entered my head.

'Why not?'

Mrs Simmonds, irritated by my nerve at daring to ask the question, pursued her lips. Eventually she said, 'I should never have let you start visiting him in the first place. I knew no good would come of it. Adam was getting along quite nicely until you came along.'

I hadn't the slightest idea what she was getting at. 'What have I done?'

'You've got Adam all stirred up, that's what you've done!' she said bitterly. 'Just when he was starting to calm down again after the move, too. You've known him for five minutes and you think you know all the answers. We've always had a birthday tea for Adam and you can come to that,' she added grudgingly.

'But what's so wrong with a special outing as well?'

Suddenly, from behind Mrs Simmonds, a man spoke. 'I

think the girl's got a point, Maggie,' he said softly.

It was only when he spoke I realised, the whole time I'd been there, Mr Simmonds had been quietly getting on with his tea at the kitchen table.

It wasn't surprising I hadn't noticed him. Even when I *knew* he was there, Mr Simmonds was hard to spot!

Unlike his colourful wife, Mr Simmonds' dusty, blue boiler-suit was the most colourful thing about him. He had more eyebrows than hair, and they were silver. The pupils of his eyes were so grey, they all but merged with the whites.

My relief at discovering an ally was short-lived as Mrs Simmonds immediately swung round and attacked him. 'I might have expected you'd take her side!' she shouted at him.

Not being used to family arguments, I instantly considered the possibility of using sheer will-power to prise open the black and white tiles of the kitchen floor, so that my body could quietly slip through into the welcoming earth beneath.

But Mr Simmonds didn't bother to raise his voice. 'I'm not taking sides,' he said reasonably. 'I just think it's a nice idea for Adam and it's very kind of . . .er . . .?'

'Anne,' I offered.

' . . . very kind of Anne to go to the trouble of arranging it.'

'She hasn't arranged it!' Mrs Simmonds snapped back. 'She does the easy part. It's me that's left with the worry of getting him there and back. Not to mention all the sorting out afterwards,' she added darkly.

Mr Simmonds, having finished his meal, carefully laid his knife and fork down and adjusted their angle a couple of times before he spoke. 'Maggie, you take too much on. We'll all help, won't we, Anne?'

'Yes, of course,' I agreed eagerly. 'The cinema manager

said he didn't mind how many of us came.'

When I'd first thought of the idea, I'd had visions of Adam and I going alone, until I quickly realised that unless I wanted to push him through the streets in his transport bubble, which would have been faintly embarrassing for everyone, we needed help. Adam's parents were the only people I knew (apart from all of Mel's boyfriends!) with a car. So I'd included them in my original invitation.

Mrs Simmonds threw the dishcloth she'd been holding into the sink. 'Well, I can see it doesn't matter what I think. Between you, you've got it all decided,' she snapped and stomped off towards the door. 'Do whatever you like, I'm having nothing more to do with it.' And she swept out, slamming the door behind her.

After she'd gone, the silence she left behind was large enough to fill a swimming pool. I knew if I didn't break it Mr Simmonds wouldn't and we'd still be there in a hundred years time, mummified. 'Mr Simmonds, I really didn't mean to cause any trouble,' I apologised.

He let out a sigh, which half sounded like relief. 'Don't worry. Maggie'll come round to it in the end. The trouble is, she wears herself out worrying about Adam.'

He looked pretty exhausted himself, but it didn't seem tactful to mention it. 'I can understand that.'

'It was very kind of you to think of doing something for Adam's birthday, but if you'll excuse me,' he said, getting up from the table and carrying his empty plate over to the draining-board, 'I've got to get back to work.'

'Yes, of course. I've got to be going anyway.'

Standing up, he didn't look nearly so weedy. He towered above me and had muscular arms and hands, which made it all the more curious that he handled his wife, whom he was obviously capable of snapping in two with his bare hands, with kid gloves. But his voice stayed gentle and polite. 'Aren't you going to go through and tell Adam?'

'Maybe some other time,' I said and fled.

But I never got the chance to tell Adam.

Later that evening I had him burbling at me down the phone. 'How did you fix it?'

I tried to play innocent. 'Fix what?'

'The cinema visit for my birthday.'

I couldn't believe it! 'How do you know about that?'

'It is true, isn't it?'

'Yes, but it was supposed to be a surprise. Who told you?'

'Mum, just now.'

I thought that was really ripe! The very person who'd kicked up holy hell about the idea had pinched the pleasure of breaking the news to Adam! 'What did she say about going?' I asked cautiously.

'Just that it was going to happen.'

'I suppose she didn't mention the fuss she made when I first asked her?'

Adam sounded puzzled. 'No.'

'You'd have thought I wanted to get you to kick off at the Wembley Cup Final.'

'Oh, that's just Mum's way. She always gets all worked up when anything new's suggested.'

'Your dad was more in favour than she was.'

'Really?' Adam sounded genuinely surprised.

'He's all right, your dad.'

'I suppose. I don't see very much of him.'

'He seems to work very hard.'

'It's not just that. Sometimes I think he sees me as some sort of cross he has to bear through life.'

'What makes you say that?'

'Dad was a great athlete and all-round sportsman when he was a kid, captain of his school's soccer and cricket First Elevens. He even had trials with professional soccer clubs and he kept on playing, right up until I was born.'

'Why did he stop – too much work?'

'So he says, but I don't believe him. I think he blames himself for my illness.'

'That's rubbish. It's nobody's fault.'

'Try telling him that!' Adam said. 'Mum says, from the moment he first heard that SCID was caused by a genetic deficiency, he believed he was the one responsible. Which means he sees me as some kind of reflection on his manhood! That's why he flogs himself to death earning the extra money to support me, which also gives him a good excuse for never being around so he doesn't have to see me.'

'That's not very fair,' I said. 'He can't be in two places at once.'

'No, but the further away from me he is, the happier he is. You've got to understand, having been such a very physical person all his life, we've nothing in common and Dad just doesn't know how to deal with me.'

'You say that, but he was all in favour of the idea of going to the cinema. It was your mother who was dead against it.'

'Yes, but I bet you anything, come Wednesday, Dad won't be there.'

'I think you're being unfair.'

'Okay, wait and see. I'd better go now, but thanks for thinking of it, I think it's a brilliant idea. By the way, what's the film called?'

Horror struck me. 'I'm sorry, I completely forgot to ask. I was so thrilled when the manager finally agreed, I never bothered to ask what was showing.'

'Don't worry. I don't mind. It could be *Bambi* for all I care. Just being inside a real cinema for the first time will be thrill enough for me.'

When Adam rang off I continued to agonise over the choice of film. Suppose it was something horrendously unsuitable? If it turned out to be the heartrending tale of a boy dying young from some terrible disease, I'd probably jump off the balcony, if they had one!

Then, and worse still, I suddenly realised that, with all the fuss Mrs Simmonds had made, I had completely forgotten to mention the price Adam was expected to pay for admission – having his photograph taken for the newspaper.

In the end I decided, having finally got Mrs Simmonds to agree, it was probably best forgotten and with any luck the manager might forget too!

When, bubbling with excitement, I rang Mel to break the news, she came right down to basics. 'So what are you going to wear?'

'What does it matter?'

'Of course it matters,' Mel insisted. 'After all, it is your *first* real date, you've got to make it special.'

I argued for playing the whole thing down. 'It's hardly a night out at the End of the Rainbow disco! Anyway, how do *you* decide what to wear for your dates?'

'I always choose something that tones with the colour of their cars.'

'Thanks a lot,' I said, 'that really helps! If I followed your example, with Adam in the transport bubble, I'd end up wearing a see-through top!'

'Only if you want to frighten the poor lad to death!'

'Charming!'

In the end we spent all of Saturday raiding every boutique in the shopping centre. I frantically tried on everything from gold stretch Lurex boob tubes, which made me look like a Christmas cracker, to slinky mini-skirts. But whatever I chose, I still ended up looking like a gift-wrapped broom handle.

Finally I settled on something which I believed most nearly matched my personality – smart but understated. A baggy sweatshirt in deep, deep purple to wear with some baggy black jeans.

Mel wasn't convinced. 'All that purple and black makes you look a bit like the Archbishop of Canterbury off to an exorcism.'

But, apart from the colour, mostly I liked the way the outfit concealed the fact that I'm obviously a direct descendant of a stick insect.

When Wednesday came, it turned out that the problem of the photograph and the choice of film, were the least of my worries, because Adam's prediction came true.

With the connivance of Miss Weinstock, who was prepared to agree that going with Adam was an essential part of my project, I'd arranged a morning away from school. But at seven o'clock on Wednesday morning the phone rang. It was Mrs Simmonds, who simply said, and I swear I could hear the triumph in her voice, 'I'm afraid today's excursion will have to be cancelled.'

I might have known she'd kill the idea off one way or another. Resisting the temptation to scream at her down the phone, I coldly asked, 'Why?'

'Mr Simmonds can't get time off work,' she said smugly, 'and without another adult present, I'm afraid I wouldn't be able to cope.'

'Oh, I see. Well, thanks for telling me.'

My mother, who was just leaving the house and who'd been as excited as me about the whole idea, could clearly see I was devastated. 'What's happened?'

I explained, adding bitterly, 'She's been against the idea from the very beginning. I wouldn't put it past her to have rung her husband's boss and *made* him say Mr Simmonds had to work!'

'Never mind that,' Mum said. 'Ring Mrs Simmonds back and tell her it's on again. I'll do it.'

'But what about your job?'

'I'll ring the office and tell them I've got to have the day off because I'm suffering from galloping follicles.'

'Sounds nasty – what on earth are galloping follicles?'

'Over-productive hair roots,' Mum said with a wicked grin, 'but I doubt they'll know that!'

'Mum, you're fantastic!' I said, hugging her hard enough to strangle anybody's follicles.

'Ring Mrs Simmonds quickly before she goes out, or something.'

I did, carefully suppressing my pleasure. 'Have you told Adam yet about not going to the cinema?'

'No,' she said suspiciously.

'Good, because you won't have to now. You said it couldn't be done without two adults, well, my mother's agreed to help. We'll be round at ten to ten, if that's okay.'

To give Mrs Simmonds her due, once she realised she was beaten, she gave in gracefully. Or at least, as gracefully as she could after her Size 16 body had been shoe-horned into a pair of Size 12, lime green, stretch Crimplene slacks.

Adam, looking fantastic in a mossy green, open-necked shirt and jeans, was already sitting in the transport bubble when we arrived.

'Happy Birthday,' I said, before realising that, while he was in there without a speaker, apart from shouting, there was no way we could communicate. But really there was no need. Adam and I were so pleased with ourselves, because it was actually happening, we just grinned at each other like a pair of idiots.

I held the air cylinder, while Mum and Mrs Simmonds struggled to slide Adam's portable tent into the back of their battered estate car. After the chrome-plated trolley was strapped to the roof-rack, I crawled in alongside Adam and we set off.

• • •

During the journey across town, Adam tried to look really laid back, as if this was an everyday experience. Only the way his eyes darted eagerly back and forth, drinking in every little detail, gave him away and I began to understand how caged in and deprived he really was.

By the time we were wheeling the bubble across the cinema foyer's vast marbled floor, the look of sheer wonderment on his face was more like that of a six-year-old on his first visit to the zoo. Except, in this case, some of the cinemagoers were staring at Adam so much, he might easily have been mistaken for a rare species arriving.

Fortunately Adam was far too busy gazing round himself to notice them.

Remembering how I'd first reacted, I suppose you could hardly blame them. We were an odd quartet. Three harpies, of varying shapes and ages, one with a delirious grin all over her face, wheeling in a travelling greenhouse containing a fully grown boy. To them he must have looked like a cannibal's pre-packed, boil-in-the-bag snack! At least, if he'd been wearing a spacesuit, they might have dismissed it as some zany publicity stunt for *Alien 9*.

The cinema manager was the only person who accepted the whole thing as if it was an everyday occurrence. With a fixed smile on his face, he glided towards us across the marble floor as smoothly as if he were on casters and waved casually with a half-bow, as if Adam were the Crown Prince arriving in a royal coach. Without pausing for an acknowledgement, he swept us into the cinema, down the centre aisle and right into the front row.

Although that didn't please Mrs Simmonds, 'I'm sure I'll get one of my headaches being this close,' it was a skilfully chosen position. While the sloping floor gave the newspaper people a clear view of the screen over Adam's greenhouse, we could sit in seats either side of the bubble – which pleased me enormously.

Without wishing to get involved in a brawl with Mrs Simmonds, I was prepared to murder to sit next to Adam. This way, with an empty seat in the middle behind the bubble, she and I could sit either side, with my mother in the aisle seat on my left.

I think that day must have won a prize for the weirdest first date in history! Here we were, not only chastely separated by a thick sheet of polythene, but out with two chaperones!

Adam didn't care where we sat. He was far too busy staring at what, I discovered later, was the largest room he'd ever been inside.

'Happy now?' Mum whispered to me as the lights dimmed.

'For sure!' I said and meant it.

Nor need I have worried about the choice of film. It turned out to be the latest in a long line of Stallone vigilante movies. Too noisy and violent for my taste, but despite there being a death every ten seconds, these happily owed more to agile stunt men, fiery special effects and gory make-up than to real life.

Stallone's main objective appeared to be to totally destroy, in an hour and a half, one of the Third World countries the rest of us have spent years trying to rebuild with our donations to Oxfam.

It was strange to think that the gung-ho story on the screen certainly wasn't the only one unfolding in the cinema that morning, though curiously it was the most believable.

Far more dramatic, for me, was the sensation of sitting with Adam in that darkened cinema, knowing that, in spite of this being his sixteenth birthday, it was the first time he'd ever seen a film on a big screen.

During the film, Adam spent as much time tracing the source of the images on the screen, back to the hole in the projection-room wall, as he did watching them. Fortunately there was little meaningful dialogue and the sound effects were easily loud enough to blast their way through to Adam.

As soon as the lights went down, Adam attracted my attention by gently tapping on the side wall. He pointed down to his palm, lying against the side wall, which I covered with mine.

Although it was far away from the graphic accounts of her skirmishes in the back-row double seats Mel had so often given me, to me this day was far more special.

And I discovered, when the film ended, and while we were still blinking in the unfamiliar light, I wasn't the only person who thought Adam was far more interesting than anyone who'd appeared on the screen.

Suddenly Mum, Mrs Simmonds and I were all roughly elbowed aside, as a rugby scrum of journalists and photographers jostled for places around Adam.

'What's going on?' demanded Mrs Simmonds.

Ashamed that I hadn't warned her about the publicity photographs, I blushed as the motor-driven cameras whirred. At that moment I wished the flashes from their cameras were bolts of lightning, which would strike me down; that way I wouldn't have to confess and face her justified anger.

'I'm sorry,' I mumbled, 'I forgot to tell you, the manager said he wanted a photograph to mark the occasion. But I honestly didn't think it would turn out like this.!'

Mrs Simmonds' face was purple with rage. 'Well, I hope you're satisfied! Ever since Adam was born, being made an exhibition of is what I've tried to protect him from.'

I turned away from her, but got no comfort from the look in Adam's soft, dark eyes, which displayed all the resignation of a trapped animal.

9

The journey back to the Simmonds' house certainly wasn't the moment to chat about the artistic display of Stallone's pectorals. It was so silent, like being in a hearse, leading a funeral procession, for which Adam's transport bubble stood in for the coffin. The body, though far from dead, deliberately avoided my eyes, which were pleading for forgiveness.

'Thank you for your help,' Mrs Simmonds said tersely to my mother, after they'd unloaded Adam and wheeled him back to the house. Then, totally ignoring me, she simply closed the door.

'I blew it, didn't I?' I said, as we wandered home together. 'It was supposed to be an experience of a lifetime for Adam.'

'Oh, I think it was that all right,' Mum said quietly.

'But not in that way!'

'Did you know all those photographers were going to be there?'

'Well, not so many, but at least one, yes,' I admitted. 'I know I should have mentioned it before we went, but I didn't want to give Mrs Simmonds the slightest excuse for calling it off. You saw how she grabbed at the chance of cancelling the moment she knew Mr Simmonds wasn't going to be around.'

'Even so,' Mum said, 'I think she's got good reason to be upset.'

'Adam wasn't exactly thrilled either. Did you see his

face? I was supposed to be going to go round for the birthday tea, but in the circumstances I think I'd better stay as far away from the Simmonds' household as possible for a while. I doubt Mrs Simmonds would bother to open the door, the mood she's in at the moment.'

So I didn't go to the tea, spent a miserable evening wondering if Adam had managed to enjoy any of his birthday and wishing I'd never dreamt up the cinema idea in the first place.

Why had I tried to be so clever? I should have stuck to buying him a daft card and something really useless, that he'd probably never actually receive, like a packet of handkerchiefs.

All evening I hoped the phone would ring, that it would be Adam to say he'd forgiven me, not that I thought he would.

So when it did ring finally at ten o'clock, I fell across the room and started apologising to Adam before he had a chance to scream at me.

Eventually I jabbered and grovelled myself to a standstill with, 'I'm sorry, I never meant it to be like that!'

'Hello, Mel Lifluous here.'

'Oh, it's you!'

'What was all that about? You didn't try to have your wicked way with the poor lad? Not on a first date! Have you no shame?'

'Oh, shut up, Mel!' Then I burst into floods of tears and eventually, after a long time, when I'd calmed down a bit, I poured out the whole story.

The difficulty was, Mel didn't know Adam, or Mrs Simmonds, nearly as well as I did. 'If you ask me I think they're both off their trolleys, if you'll pardon the expression, and making a big fuss about nothing.'

'She's so protective towards Adam. I can understand it in

the practical sense. The slightest germ, something that we'd never even notice, could kill him. So in many ways he's lucky to be alive. It's mostly thanks to her that he is, but she's so over-protective, she rules his entire life. I know Adam was upset, but I'm sure that's mainly because she's kept him hidden away all this time. Look at the way she didn't want us to have classes with Adam. I bet they never would have happened if Miss Weinstock hadn't insisted. Sometimes I think Mrs Simmonds would like to lock Adam away.'

'Like Mr Rochester did with his mad wife in *Jane Eyre*,' Mel suggested.

'Wow! And I've always said the only thing you ever read was *What Car*?! No, but you know what I mean. Mrs Simmonds wants to keep him all to herself and she can't bear the idea of anyone else doing anything for him.'

'I still can't see what harm having his photograph in the local paper is going to do. That reminds me,' Mel suddenly said, 'that's why I rang in the first place.'

'What is?'

'Did I ever tell you Rob's a photographer?'

'No, I thought he just drove round in a Porsche all day waiting for you.'

Mel ignored me. 'Well, he is and he wants to do some photographs of me.'

'So?'

'Proper ones, in a studio and everything. He says the camera will love me because I've got magnificent bone structure.'

Bones being my strongest feature, I couldn't help wondering why nobody ever pleaded to photograph me. Maybe it had something to do with the fact that while my cheekbones looked as if they were about to puncture my skin, Mel's, which were every bit as prominent, are neatly padded like a baby's clenched fist.

'Rob says I ought to be a model.'

'What for – high-rise buildings with big balconies?'

'A photographic model – fashion.'

'You want to watch out for him, Mel. He'll be telling you soon he can get you into films.'

'No, it's straight up. He wants to do some shots and show them to an agency he works for.'

'Are you serious?'

Mel sounded hurt. 'You don't believe me, do you? Lots of girls younger than me do it. You know that Belgian pop singer, Vanessa Paradis? She was already a famous model by the time she was fourteen.'

'Too bad you're already over the hill!'

'These days, half the girls on the cover of *Vogue* are under eighteen. You can earn a fortune.'

'You could even buy your own Porsche.'

'I'm being serious!' She suddenly sounded it too. 'Do you think I ought to do it?'

'Why not. Go for it, I say!'

'Would you come with me?'

Although we'd gone around together, Mel had never in her life taken me with her when she had a man in tow. 'What on earth for?'

'Rob says he's going to borrow all sorts of outfits for me from designers he knows. It could be a great laugh.'

'But you won't need me there,' I said. To be honest the novelty was already wearing off and my mind was really more on Adam than what Mel was saying.

But she was strangely insistent, almost pleading with me, which sounded odd coming from somebody as sure of herself as Mel. 'Anne, I'd really like you to be there.'

'I can't see why.'

'Remember what you said when I first told you, about him telling me he could get me into pictures? Well, the same thought crossed my mind too. Don't get me wrong.

Rob is a really nice guy and I know you think I sometimes behave like a bit of a slag, but I'm not stupid and I'm not going into this with my eyes shut.'

'Okay, Mel, I'll be there, if you want me to.'

'Thanks. I'll let you know when we fix a date.'

'Don't worry, I don't expect my engagement diary will get too crowded over the next few weeks!'

'I think you ought to look at the paper,' Mum said the following day when I came down for breakfast.

Staring up at me was a black and white image of Adam, made somehow surreal by the light of the electronic flashes bouncing off the plastic, which left him looking as if he was trapped inside a giant aquarium. 'But it's only Thursday, I thought the local paper didn't come out until tomorrow.'

'It doesn't. That's the daily paper. Somehow they've got hold of the photograph too.'

The moment I got to school, copies of all the tabloids and several 'serious' papers, all of which carried pictures of Adam, were waved under my nose.

After a couple of half-hearted attempts I gave up trying to explain why I wasn't excited. They were all thrilled skinny (never an expression I've personally approved of!) that somebody *they* knew was in all the papers. They couldn't have been more pleased if one of us had been turned overnight into a pop star. They couldn't understand, and frankly didn't care, how Adam, or I, felt about him being plastered everywhere.

In fact Mum and I only appeared, very fuzzy, lurking in the background of some of the pictures, with me doing my famous impersonation of a Tasmanian Devil.

Although I could hardly bear to look at them, I kept all the newspaper clippings for my project. The most amazing thing about them were the captions and, worse still, the headlines. They were littered with simple inaccuracies, they gave the wrong age, they spelt his surname with one 'm'. Most of the captions lip-smacked heavily over the idea of Adam's death, which they tactfully implied was likely any second, if not overdue!

One editor, with the sensitivity of an earth-moving machine, wrote, in 20mm black capitals: DYING BOY'S DAY OUT.

Only the serious papers bothered to name Adam's actual illness, while some of the tabloids managed to give the impression Adam had to be kept under wraps to protect us from *him*, rather than the other way round!

I was beginning to see exactly what Mrs Simmonds was so anxious to protect her son from.

I also got a hint of the downside of fame, even if mine was only fame by association.

From the moment I got home the phone never stopped ringing. If it wasn't a friend, or a distant relation, including several I'd never heard of, saying, 'Have you seen your picture in the paper?', it was a journalist from one of the tabloids, lip-smacking as he pleaded for more gory details about Adam.

Knowing a good sob-story could boost their sales figures nearly as high as a royal scandal, they all wanted to publish follow-up articles. Perhaps through the cinema manager, they'd found out the whole thing was my idea, so now it was me they were after! But knowing the way Mrs Simmonds felt about the whole business I was determined to say nothing and swore I was my sister. 'You can't talk to Anne,' I said to one, 'she's in the bath.'

But that wasn't good enough. They simply insisted on ringing back. So, out of desperation, I resorted to the outlandish. 'I'm afraid Anne's busy trepanning herself at the moment and, if I interrupt, the electric drill could slip and pierce her brain.'

I couldn't believe it when, after a moment's silence, the

man asked, in all seriousness, 'Could you spell trepanning for me?'

'I'm not sure what worries me most,' I complained to Mum, 'the fact that he believed me, or that someone who writes for the newspapers is illiterate!'

Eventually, if only to preserve my sanity and avoid dying of starvation, I took the phone off the hook for the rest of the evening. I didn't replace it until after ten, when it immediately rang again.

'Go away and leave me alone!' I shrieked into the receiver.

'What have I done wrong now?' Adam asked.

'Oh, it's you!'

'Anne, what on earth's the matter?'

'If you've rung up to tell me off, let me tell you, nothing you can say could make me feel worse than I already do!'

'Tell you off? Why should I want to do that?' Adam sounded genuinely puzzled.

Was I hearing right? 'About your picture being in all the papers.'

'Isn't it great?' he laughed.

'Great?!'

'I'm famous.'

'Well, when I last saw you, you certainly didn't look as pleased as you sound now.'

'That was before I realised how interesting I am.'

This was marvellous! For the past twenty-four hours, I'd gone into hiding while I agonised over what I'd done and here he was, sounding as if he'd just been awarded a Nobel Prize. Worse, whilst I'd accepted the blame for what had happened, he was happily taking all the credit!

Adam proudly told me, 'Today Mum did an in-depth interview for the *Guardian* and tomorrow there's someone coming to see me from the *Lancet*.'

'The *Lancet*?'

'Yes, you know, the medical journal. They say I'm unique.'

'Oh, you're that all right!' I said heavily.

'What's up with you, you sound really grouchy?'

To give him his due, after I'd explained what I'd been going through, he did apologise, adding, 'But, Anne, yours was the best, most exciting, birthday present I've ever had.' A tiny glow of pride began to filter through my veins as Adam continued, 'Wasn't that place fantastic? I've never been inside anywhere nearly as big as that. Did you notice all those tiny little lights, like stars, scattered all over the ceiling? And the size of the screen! I'd never imagined they were that big. It makes watching videos on the TV more like peeping through a letterbox.'

'I'm sorry we didn't get a better choice of film.'

'It was okay. Mind you, I would have preferred a Western.'

'Don't tell me you're into all that macho cowboys and Indians stuff!'

'What's wrong with that?'

Adam was so cut off from everyday life, sometimes he seemed a bit naive and not always politically correct!

Apart from which, it seemed such an odd choice. 'What is it about Westerns that turns you on?'

'Isn't it obvious? All the things I can't share. The great outdoors, riding horses off into the sunset. I'd love to do that,' Adam said wistfully.

'I see what you mean.'

'I love all the classics, like *High Noon* and all those Clint Eastwood spaghetti-Westerns. Incidentally, did you know the idea that all Red Indians took scalps is completely wrong?'

'No, Adam, oddly enough, I didn't.'

'Originally only two tribes, the Crees and the Teton Dakotas, took scalps. It was against all the Navahos' traditions to touch anything that was dead, even one of their enemies. The idea of scalping only spread after the Dutch, and later the English, started paying a bounty for every Red Indian scalp handed in. Amazing, isn't it? Even as late as 1866, you could get still $250 for a scalp in Arizona.'

He was always full of that sort of stuff! 'And I suppose that's where the expression, "keep your hair on", comes from?'

'Ha-ha!'

'So how was the rest of your birthday?' I asked, with pangs of jealousy, because I hadn't been there to enjoy it with him, not that he seemed to have noticed.

'Fine, I didn't cut the cake until Dad got home.'

'You have a birthday cake?'

'Yes,' he said, 'but that's fairly new. I was twelve before I got my first one, after they found a vacuum-packed, tinned cake that was safe for me to eat. At least I'm allowed to cut it now, and send pieces out for them, but Mum still keeps the candles outside and blows them out with Dad.'

'And I bet she makes your wish for you too.'

'Don't be daft.'

'Has she calmed down yet, about the photographers?'

'She's not as pleased as I am, but she's coming round.'

'Which is more than I am, coming round, I mean.'

'Why not?'

'Not until all this has died down.'

'But you've got to, I cut a piece of cake specially for you.'

Strange isn't it? They always say, it's the thought that counts. Just knowing Adam had cut that piece of cake for me, that there was something which he'd touched, waiting for me, turned my knees to the strength and consistency of hot jam.

10

None of us could have realised the enormous changes in our lives which would eventually come out of those first pictures appearing, but things certainly went a little crazy!

For quite a while hardly a week went by without either an article on Adam, or another picture, appearing in something or other. He even made the cover of *Hello*.

So much was happening that Mrs Simmonds couldn't make up her mind how to react. One minute she'd be complaining bitterly about never getting a moment's peace. The next she was basking in the reflected glory, which was particularly true when *Woman* ran a whole article on the sacrifices she'd made in her life to look after Adam. To top that she was nominated as a *Mum of the Year*.

Round about then she asked my mum to paint Adam's portrait. Mrs Simmonds had found out while they were chatting during the cinema trip, that Mum was an artist. She just assumed Mum was that kind of painter. What she didn't realise was that my mother's style was rather more Picasso than that and Adam might end up with a leg growing out of his ear!

'I haven't drawn anyone since I was at Art School,' Mum said, when I passed on the news of Mrs Simmonds' commission.

'Give it a try,' I suggested. 'I'd like a picture of Adam, especially one done by you.'

'Why doesn't she get a portrait photographer round? I'm sure that's much more the sort of thing she wants.'

'An oil painting in a huge gilt frame that makes Adam look like Son of the Laughing Cavalier, is what she wants.'

Mum slowly shook her head. 'She may think that now, but later, if you see what I mean, she'd probably hate it. I mean, if anything happens to Adam, after he's gone, the last thing she'll want is to have him hanging permanently on her wall in glorious living colour. Oil paintings of your ancestors are all very well when they're long gone, after a decent, or even disreputable, life.'

The enormity of what Mum was saying suddenly struck me. 'You sound as bad as those blood-sucking journalists, you think he's going to die, don't you?'

'Anne, calm down! We all are.'

'But in Adam's case, you think it's going to happen sooner, rather than later.'

Mum looked uncomfortable. 'You've known all along that he has a big problem, there's no use pretending otherwise. That means . . .'

'I don't want to hear what that means!' I shouted at her and covered my ears.

Mum put her arms round me. I tried to shrug her off, but she wouldn't let me. 'I just think it would be . . . kinder to yourself, if you kept that in the back of your mind.'

But I refused to listen to that kind of defeatist talk. 'Something will happen, you'll see. With all the tests they do, they're bound to come up with a cure.'

'Yes, they might,' she agreed.

'So, let's leave it like that, okay?'

Mum smiled gently. 'If that's what you want.'

'It is. Now, what about this picture.'

'I tell you what I'll do. I won't commit myself yet, but I'll go round, try some sketches and see how they work out. Do you think Adam will mind sitting for me?'

'I'm sure he'll love it. Like he always says, "It's not as if I'm going anywhere else." Besides, with all the photographers who've been hanging round him lately, posing is becoming second nature to him.'

Quite a change had come over Adam since his photograph appeared in the newspaper and it wasn't one that I particularly liked. He'd got very full of himself. Don't get me wrong, I was pleased that some of the old uncertainty had gone, but now the pendulum had swung too far in the opposite direction. For someone who wasn't allowed to wear shoes, for fear of piercing the plastic, he was getting far too big for his socks.

But I really thought he'd gone totally ballistic when I went round to see him one day and he announced, 'I'm going to be a star!'

'You what?'

'This morning I got a call from a man who's read all about me in the papers and wants to make a TV mini-series based on my life.'

'Move over Martin Luther King and John F. Kennedy,' I said, already in training for the Sarcasm Olympics, 'this could be the big one!'

Totally unable to see the funny side, he was hurt. 'I thought you'd be pleased for me.'

'Of course I am.'

'Who do you think they'll get to play me? I thought, for when I was little, it could be Macaulay Culkin out of *Home Alone* and then maybe Jason Donovan for when I'm older.'

'Aren't they both blond?'

'Oh, of course they'd have to dye their hair, but I'm sure they wouldn't mind doing a little thing like that, not if it meant they could play me.'

He was serious! 'And who had you in mind to play me?' I asked casually.

Adam looked totally blank. 'You?'

'I do appear in this multi-million dollar extravaganza,

don't I? I mean, not so long ago, you gave me the impression I was quite important in your life.'

He swallowed and thought quickly. He'd been so busy thinking about himself, my role had obviously never crossed his mind. 'Of course you do.'

'Played by who – Madonna?'

'You're mad! She's far too . . .'

'Sexy?'

'Old, that's what I was going to say, far too old.'

Maybe he was right. Perhaps he no longer needed me, not now he was famous. Since the photographs appeared he'd had stacks of letters from girls. Everything from perfectly harmless pen pals to decidedly more sleazy offers. One of his groupies had even sent a photograph of herself, wearing a bikini, which was clearly visible with the aid of a powerful magnifying glass!

At first I'd been given the doubtful honour of reading them to him and we'd laughed about them together. But then, when he began to suspect I was editing them (well, there was a limit to how much gush I could cope with!), he suddenly changed his mind, insisted they were all sterilised and sent for him to read. After that, he rarely mentioned the contents.

It was round about that time I was appointed to my new role as his Official Taster. I've no idea whether this was sparked off by the trip to the cinema, his new-found fame, or the letters, but suddenly he wanted me to tell him how it felt to do the weirdest things.

Some were simple and I'd already tried them, like explaining the taste of curry. Others, like walking barefoot, at dawn, through dew-laden grass (I bet that came from the over-inflated blonde in the devalued bikini!) were things I had to go out and try specially, then struggle to explain to him what they'd felt like.

One of the earliest, and most uncomfortable, sprang from Adam's obsession with Westerns. He insisted I should go for a gallop on a horse.

'I've never even ridden a donkey on the sands,' I protested.

'But it looks so easy.'

'That's in films, Adam,' I pointed out. 'Getting a car to go along on its side on two wheels looks pretty easy on film, but I bet the stuntmen who do it start with ordinary driving lessons and build up gradually. They don't just leap into the first car they see and up-end it!'

Adam looked bitterly disappointed. 'So you'd rather not do it?'

'Oh, all right, but only on condition that I don't have to a) ride side-saddle or bare-back, b) dress as a cowgirl, or c) carry six-shooters.'

'You could go as a squaw,' he suggested.

'There is no way . . .'

'I was only joking.'

The woman at the riding centre was horrified when I explained why I'd come. 'Gallop?' she boomed at me. 'Your first priority is to find out if you can stay on a horse. It'll probably take more than half a dozen lessons to give you a decent seat.'

A decent seat, being more bone than flesh, was exactly what I lacked and I was forced to deliver my first report to Adam standing up, having returned from my lesson with my rear end more battered than a tenderised steak.

I never did get to gallop. My animal appeared to have been fitted with an automatic ejector seat. The first time it broke into a canter I found myself sitting on the grass. But at least I was able to tell Adam how it felt to have the wind in my face, even if I left out the more painful part about the ground rising up to meet me.

The experiences weren't all bad. I enjoyed going on a

Thames pleasure-boat and I didn't even object to throwing up over the people watching me at the fairground, when I sampled the white-knuckle torture of going round on the Corkscrew.

It was the Saturday evening as I returned from that trip, still an unusual shade of green, when I walked unsteadily into our house and found my father waiting for me!

I'd always kept a fading photograph of him, which Mum had given me, on my desk.

If we ever had a horrendous row, I would gaze longingly at it and fantasize about him returning, having made his first million, and carrying me off to a far better life!

Most of the time though, it just sat there, gathering dust, though a day never went by without me looking at this absent stranger and, as I grew older, realising that I was starting to look more and more like him.

And now, suddenly, after all those years of wondering about him and how different my life might have been if he hadn't disappeared, there he was. Sixteen years later and still looking exactly the same. Surely, I thought, I must be hallucinating. How could he still look the same after all those years? Maybe he was not of this world? A spirit visitation perhaps?

Mum, with a smudge of blue paint on one cheek, not only looked amazingly calm, but very down-to-earth about the whole business. 'Anne, I'd like you to meet . . .'

'I know who he is.'

'You must be thinking what I thought when I answered the doorbell,' Mum said. 'But this is Uncle Graham, your father's younger brother.' The explanation was very simple. Having lost touch during the years my mother and I moved from address to address, Uncle Graham had finally tracked us down after recognising Mum's shadowy figure in one of Adam's newspaper pictures.

'Why didn't my father come?' I asked.

Mum slowly walked across the room and slipped an arm round my shoulder. 'He couldn't, love. He died eight years ago.'

Illogically, I tried to remember what I was doing when I was eight. A curious mixture of sadness and anger erupted inside me, but what I mostly suffered was an awful emptiness, that and a huge sense of being cheated.

Though I couldn't remember him and he'd abandoned us, until that moment, irrational as the idea was, it seemed to me there had always been the possibility that one day, somehow, all the thoughts and feelings I'd had about him could be sorted out. Now that was suddenly wiped out. He'd abandoned me again. And this time it really was for ever.

It just didn't seem fair!

Even the method of death was so casual. You'd have thought at least he might have had the decency to make the whole thing worthwhile by dying fighting for queen and country, or saving someone else's life, by wrestling with an alligator in the Florida swamps, but no.

'He fell under a train in Edinburgh,' Graham explained.

Obviously even Mum, having struggled as a single parent all my life, had hoped for something more dramatic than that. 'Was he drunk?'

Graham smiled gently. 'No. The platform was slippery, somebody tripped and fell against him, pushing him under the wheels.'

'Poor John,' Mum said quietly and then looked puzzled. 'What on earth was he doing in Edinburgh?'

'He was on his way up to Aberdeen. He worked for an oil company and had to visit one of the rigs.'

By now the anger had boiled away. This was a complete stranger I was hearing about. The person who bumped into him on the platform, causing his death, probably knew more about him than I did. Nothing I'd ever heard about my father suggested somebody who might have worked on oil-rigs. Even in his photograph he looked so slender. It turned out he'd become an industrial chemist!

'When I saw your picture, I thought I ought to come and tell you what had happened to him,' Graham said.

'It was very kind of you,' Mum replied.

'I don't know why he bothered,' I grumbled, after Graham had left me in a total state of anti-climax.

Maybe that was partly relief. While they'd been talking I had slowly started to realise that, after all those years, Mum and I being so close, I might not have adjusted very well to the sudden arrival of an instant father, who was in reality a total stranger. It could have been more traumatic than getting a stepfather. A new uncle, somebody who occasionally sent you birthday cards and whom you could take or leave, was much easier to cope with.

'Perhaps it's different for you,' Mum said, 'but at least it puts a genuine full stop to a chapter of my life, instead of leaving a question mark. And maybe,' she added, thoughtfully, 'it tells us something about how we ought to treat people while they're still with us and make certain we tell them the things we want them to know while we have the chance.' Mum, knowing that she didn't have to spell out her thoughts on my relationship with Adam further, went back to her painting.

But my new-found uncle wasn't the last person to turn up unexpectedly as a result of the articles on Adam.

11

'Anne, I've been thinking, you ought to go out with somebody else.'

Coming out of the blue, Adam's words left me feeling as if I'd head-butted a brick wall. 'Adam, I don't understand what you're saying. Is this supposed to be just another of my assignments as your Official Taster? Because, if it is, I don't think much of it.'

'Of course not,' Adam said, though I thought he looked a little shifty.

'Then what's your point?'

'Just because I can't lead a normal life, doesn't mean you shouldn't either.'

I'd never heard anything so stupid in my life, but I still wanted to reach out and clutch at the furniture for support. Suddenly my whole world felt destabilised by this earthquake. 'Don't I have any say in this? As it happens I'm perfectly happy with things the way they are.'

'But it isn't fair that you should be stuck in here with me all the time. For people of our age that's unreal.'

'It's the same for both of us,' I pointed out.

'I don't have any choice,' Adam replied, 'but you should be out meeting people, doing things.'

'What sort of things? Between schoolwork and seeing you, there isn't time for much else.'

'That's exactly what I'm saying and it can't be good for you.'

I looked at Adam closely. 'Is this some kind of unsubtle brush-off? "Thanks, it's been fun, but now it's over." Is that what you're really trying to say?'

'No, of course not.'

Adam sounded convincing enough, but I couldn't help noticing he was avoiding my eyes. 'So you want me to go out with somebody else?'

Adam managed an uncomfortable blush. 'Yes.'

'Okay,' I said bitterly, 'if that's the way you want it.'

But when I immediately got up to leave he looked rather startled. 'Where are you going?'

'To ring Mel and see if she'll lend me one of her spares. You know, only one previous owner, reliably road-tested and raring to go?'

I could see Adam was starting to have second thoughts. 'Anne, you're taking this the wrong way.'

'Oh, no, I've got the picture,' I said angrily as I left. I wished my mother, during one of the portrait sittings, had passed on to Adam, rather than to me, her words of wisdom about how people ought to treat one another.

With the advantage of twenty/twenty hindsight, it would certainly have been better if I'd simply refused and declared my total love for him, but I didn't. Maybe I was too hurt. Instead, I ran all the way home and rang Mel. When she asked who it was, I seethed down the line at her, 'Anne Ihilate!'

'What on earth's the matter?'

I told her roughly what Adam had said, ending with, 'So I need a new boyfriend, *now!*'

'Calm down!' Mel said. 'I think you've got this whole thing out of proportion.'

'I didn't ring up to discuss this, Mel. I've already made my decision, or at least Adam made it for me. Will you fix me up with a boyfriend from your extensive catalogue, or not? It's not as if you're using any of them while you're so busy with Rob and it seems a shame, after such thorough research, to let all that talent go rusty from lack of use.'

'Hey, take it easy! I haven't done anything to you.'

'And remember,' I said, brushing Mel aside, 'it's a sixteen-valve GTi I'm looking for, not a reliable runabout.'

'If you say so,' Mel sighed. 'I'll ring round a few people and tell you tomorrow. I suppose you can wait until then? I mean, you don't want a Lotus Elan pulling up outside your door in the next ten minutes, do you?'

'No, tomorrow will do.'

'I just hope you know what you're doing.'

'Believe me, I do!' I said and slammed the phone down. When it instantly rang, I refused to answer.

'Anne!' Mum called out. 'It's Adam for you.'

'Tell him I've gone to an orgy!'

'What?'

'Tell him I don't want to talk to him.'

I heard her murmur something into the phone and then she came into my room. 'Whatever's the matter with you two? Adam sounded very upset.'

'Nothing.'

'Nothing can't sound as bad as he did, or look as upset as you do.'

'Just leave it, okay?'

'If that's what you want,' she said, 'but if you need to talk . . .'

'I won't need to!' I snapped, but she'd barely closed the door before I threw myself on the bed, buried my face in the pillow and began to bawl.

'It wasn't easy,' Mel explained the following day at school. 'Most of the really suitable boys just don't happen to be available. Do you know, three of them actually had the nerve to tell me they were going steady with somebody else?'

94

In any other circumstances Mel's sense of outrage would have been funny.

I was neither surprised nor disappointed that nobody wanted to go out with me. Having cried myself to sleep, I'd calmed down a little. 'Mel, you don't have to make excuses.'

'Don't get crazy with me! Most were disappointed they weren't able to go out with you.'

'What choice did you give them?' I asked. 'Go out with Anne, or have your right arm chopped off?'

'No! I'm just trying to explain, one or two of my first choices weren't free.'

'Then you did finally find someone? Who did it come down to in the end?'

'Tony.'

I racked my brains. The name didn't exactly figure near the top of Mel's Car of the Year list! Then I remembered! 'Hang on a minute! He's the one you dumped after your fourth birthday party, who you've never been out with since!'

Mel avoided my eyes. 'I wouldn't say, *never* exactly.'

'When *exactly* was the last time?'

'We had a Coke together at a disco only a couple of weeks ago.'

'Even that was last year!'

Mel was genuinely surprised. 'Really? Doesn't time fly?'

'Well, thanks! You've really had to scrape the bottom of the barrel, haven't you?'

'Be fair, Anne, you didn't give me much notice. Anyway, Tony's quite a nice guy.'

'So "nice" that you never bothered to arrange a re-match with him since you were four years old!'

'Ah, but he's moved up my list since he went to college. Now he drives an E-Type Jaguar. He told me he'd picked it up cheap and rebuilt it from scratch.'

'Fascinating!'

'Look, you said you wanted an instant, blind date. So I've got you one. He's picking you up tonight at seven.'

'No, he's not. I won't go.'

'You have to,' Mel insisted. 'I told him you've always been crazy about him. It'd really hurt his feelings.'

'Ring him and tell him I'm sick.'

'For what it's worth, I think you are, in the head! But perhaps Adam's right, up to a point. Maybe it would do you good to get out once in a while, help put things between you and Adam back into perspective. And at least, with Tony, it won't be like spending the evening wrestling with an over-active octopus!'

'What do I tell Adam if he rings again?' Mum asked.

It was seven o'clock and a shiny, red and chrome monster had just cruised up to our front gate.

'Tell him I'm out on a date with Tony,' I said airily.

'I can't say that.'

'Then tell him anything you like, as long as he doesn't bother ringing me again.'

Mum gave me one of her searching looks. 'I hope you know what you're doing.'

Sometimes the freedom of action Mum permits me, places an awesome responsibility on my young, but bony shoulders. Although it would have been an all-time first for her to have forbidden me to go out with Tony, at that particular moment in history, despite a certain amount of kicking and screaming, I would have been secretly, truly grateful. It would have been like being thrown a lifeline from what suddenly seemed a very stupid act.

Tony was quite a nice guy, just as Mel had said.

A bit dull, but okay.

He was better looking, in a fairly ordinary way, than I

expected. A strong chin, black, wavy hair and serious, green eyes. But the thing which struck me most, being more used to mixing with boys of my own age at school, was how grown-up he seemed. Not so surprising when I discovered he was over four years older than me.

Expecting Tony to turn up in jeans with a spanner in his back pocket, I'd decided to play safe and go for the anonymous look. I wore an oversized black sweater over black leggings, but he wore a smart jacket, a shirt the exact shade of his eyes and slacks and suggested we went out for a Chinese meal.

Maybe it was because I wasn't remotely interested in him, but I managed to get through the whole evening without saying anything too stupid, or dribbling sweet-and-sour sauce down my chin.

Fortunately, Tony did most of the talking. The moment I'd folded myself up and climbed into his car, I'd admired it and he began a blow-by-blow account of the problems of its restoration which lasted right through to dessert. Maybe if I'd known my clutch from my carburettor I might have found it more scintillating.

'Mel would have found all that fascinating,' I said carelessly during the lychees.

His eyes lit up like undipped headlights. 'Have you known Mel long?'

'Ever since I went to the Comprehensive.'

He nodded. 'She said you were best mates. I've known her since I was little.'

'Oh, really?' I said innocently. Having spent so much time talking about cars I wasn't anxious to change the subject to Mel.

But Tony wasn't to be put off. A goofy smile spread across his face. 'I'll never forget her fourth birthday party. That was the first time I ever tasted maple and walnut jelly. Mel wore this amazing sort of purple satin romper suit. I thought she was fantastic.' Then his smile faded. 'But it turned out she'd only invited me because she wanted to borrow my new Super Scooter. It was the very latest thing with ten-inch reinforced nylon wheels and calliper brakes. But, by the time I went to the party, she'd been given some roller-boots for her birthday and my scooter was old news.'

A fast lady even at four years old!

Poor Tony! Nothing to show for all those years of dog-like devotion.

Having temporarily exhausted both his favourite topics, cars and Mel, the drive home was rather quiet but, when we pulled up outside my house, Tony sprang a double surprise on me. First of all, he asked, 'Are you doing anything Saturday evening?'

'No.' I tried to make my reply sound thoughtful, as if I wasn't totally free for the rest of my entire life.

'I wondered if you'd like to go to the cinema?'

After my most recent visit, cinemas were a rather sore subject, but perhaps this would exorcise the painful memory. 'Okay.'

'Great, I'll pick you up about half-past seven.'

I was about to climb out of the car, when he leapt out and ran round to open my door.

I was a bit knocked over. I have neatly arranged double standards about door-holding. My feminist principles make me testy when it happens, especially if I suspect they're thinking, 'Poor, weedy creature needs big, strong me to help her.' On the other hand, I really resent having doors slammed in my face. But Tony handled the whole thing so naturally, clearly intending it as a compliment, so I let it pass.

I certainly wasn't expecting him to walk me right up to my front door. 'Thanks for a nice evening,' I said, slipping my key into the lock.

'Thanks for coming,' he smiled. 'I had a great time.'

Then came the second and greatest surprise of all. Gently placing his arm round my neck, he drew me towards him and having kissed me once, full on the lips, said, 'Good night, see you Saturday!' and was gone.

As I lay in bed, I thought about Tony's kiss. It was certainly streets ahead of my first kiss behind the bike sheds all those years ago! But then, being hit in the face with an elderly, disintegrating kipper would have been a sexier experience than Darren's offering, which had left a trail of slime as if a slug had passed over my lips!

Tony obviousy knew what he was about. He hadn't lunged at me, all flailing arms, groping hands and probing tongue; though his lips had been definitely active, very firm and warm and I was left in no doubt that I *had* been kissed.

It was certainly a kiss which allowed me to consider how much I'd enjoyed it, yet just passionate enough to show the promise of far more exciting aspects to come. So, why had it had so little effect on me? Where were the promised fireworks and chiming bells? I'd experienced no weakening of the knees, or tingle down my spine.

I also bitterly resented the fact that, the moment Tony kissed me, my brain turned traitor and guiltily leapt to thoughts of Adam. I hated admitting it, but Tony's kiss was infinitely less electric than the simple touching of palms I'd experienced with Adam.

'Damn Adam!'

I thumped my pillow viciously, all the more determined to have a great time with Tony on Saturday. I vowed to encourage him, with all the limited feminine wiles at my disposal, not to stop at a mere kiss.

I fell asleep thanking my lucky stars that, with the examinations getting closer, class visits to Adam's house had been temporarily abandoned, which meant I wouldn't have to face him!

· · ·

Tony and I had been going steady for a month. Adam had finally given up trying to ring me, but Mum was still visiting him, putting the final touches to his portrait for Mrs Simmonds.

One evening, as I was about to leave for Tony's, she casually said, 'You know Adam still asks about you.'

Even the mention of his name still made my heart beat like bongo drums, but I was determined not to let it show, even to Mum. 'Does he?' I said pretending to check my hair in the hall mirror. 'Well, tell him I'm fine.'

Of course, that wasn't true. It should have been, but it wasn't.

Tony and I went everywhere together; to the cinema, autocross rallies, discos and parties. But, although we had a lot of fun, he simply wasn't Adam.

I missed Adam's stupid jokes, his zany facts, even the way he used to smile, his mouth slightly skewwhiff, when I walked into the room.

Every hour of every day Adam's name crept into my thoughts.

But I was obstinately determined to ignore those thoughts and feelings while I paid him back for pushing me away. If that was what Adam wanted, I was determined that was what he would get, with no half measures! Besides, I have to admit, although my original interest in Tony had been rather academic, there was something quite exciting about being able, for the first time in my life, to explore the range of my female powers. It was also interesting, as Tony grew more passionate with every date, trying out some of my previously unused equipment.

Take something very simple, like ears. Having wasted years believing they were given me purely so that I could hear, I quickly discovered they were, when skilfully titillated by finger or tongue, a kick-start motor for a whole kaleidoscope of new sensations.

Tony had a flat above his workshop garage and we'd begun to go out less, and stay in more and more.

Most of my free time was spent combing newspapers for film reviews. That was the only way I could keep up an intelligent discussion with Mum, about films we were supposed to have seen, but hadn't.

The flat was small, more of a bedsitter with kitchen and bathroom, and very cosy. Going there meant, if Tony was working late on a car, I could use the time to catch up on my revision.

Having suffered from years of housework, struggling to compensate for Mum's little eccentricities, one of the best things about the flat was that Tony hardly allowed me to lift a finger. The place was so clean you could have performed open-heart surgery in the kitchen. He hated mess and nothing was ever out of place. 'It wastes so much time when you can't find things.' The same rule applied to his workshop. All his tools were firmly clipped to their painted outlines on the wall and arranged in neat rows like pinned-out butterflies.

And if that wasn't enough to win him the New Man of the Year Award, Tony did all his own washing, ironing and was an excellent cook too.

'You'll make someone a terrific wife!' I laughed.

But Tony shrugged off my teasing. 'When I first went away to college I soon found out there were only three choices; starving, constantly eating at the chippie and ending up with an ulcer and zits, or learning how to cook.'

Tony treated me like a princess and although, looking back, I suppose I was only being a little girl playing house, there was a wonderful freedom about being at the flat, which I'd never enjoyed before. But I began to realise I was getting hooked on cosy domesticity the day I found myself buying a potted plant for Tony's kitchen. But then everything has its price and the day of reckoning, when I had to decide exactly what I was prepared to pay, was getting closer.

Needless to say, by then we'd moved on a good deal from that first, reasonably chaste kiss. Tony soon brought out in me sensations Mel had told me about, but which I'd never before experienced.

As the physical passion mounted, I was well aware that I was about to embark on my maiden voyage into wholly uncharted waters and the moment of, "God bless all who sail in her", was rapidly approaching!

Like any explorer, I couldn't deny I was desperately curious to know exactly what lay over the horizon. Yet every time (if you'll pardon the expression!) the chocks were about to be knocked out from under my keel, I managed to find just enough strength of will to postpone the launching.

I knew Tony loved me and I liked him, a lot, but in the end that wasn't enough. Besides, in the background, I was horribly aware that I was still only using Tony. Firstly, like a musician who wants to explore their instrument, but secondly, and far worse, as a vicious way of getting back at Adam.

Inevitably everything came to a head one night when, once again, we were about to break a metaphorical bottle of champagne over my bows. Struggling up for air, I pulled away from him. 'Tony, I'm sorry, but I can't go through with this.'

Thank God, he was very understanding. He wasn't cross, he didn't ignore me either, though he did look baffled and hurt. 'What's the matter? I thought you wanted this to happen as much as I do.'

'So did I,' I admitted quietly, 'but when it comes to the point, I know it's wrong.'

'Wrong?'

'Oh, I don't mean *wrong*, wrong! Just wrong for us.'

'But we love each other,' he declared.

'Yes, but how much?'

He was about to reply, but I stopped him by placing my finger on his lips. 'Look, if we're honest, we both know we truly love somebody else. All the time we've been seeing each other, Mel and Adam have constantly crept into our conversations.' Tony was about to protest, but I didn't let him. 'You know, if you had your *absolute* choice, this would be happening with Mel and I know I ought to be with Adam.'

'Not that I agree, but even supposing I did, neither of them is available.'

'Tony, you're a sweet, kind, considerate person. I'm very fond of you, but I happen to think we both deserve better than a consolation prize.'

'That isn't how I think of you!' he protested. 'Time changes things. Look how close we've become.'

'But those two people will always haunt us,' I insisted, 'and in the end that could ruin everything. We'd probably end up hating each other.'

'I could never hate you.'

'You can't know that.'

Poor Tony looked really miserable. 'Does this mean we're going to stop seeing each other altogether?'

I nodded. 'I think it's better that way.'

'I'll really miss you,' he sighed.

'Me too,' I said and the kiss I gave him, before I walked out of the flat for the last time, was every bit as warm and gentle as the first one he'd given me.

'You're home early,' Mum said, brightly, when I got home and wandered into her studio. 'How was the film?'

'We didn't go.'

'Oh?'

When I didn't offer to add anything she turned back to

working on Adam's portrait. It was the first time I'd seen it. Knowing what she was working on, I'd deliberately avoided going anywhere near her studio.

I was rocked back on my heels by what I saw. Far from having a leg coming out of his ear, as I'd feared and expected, it was a wonderful, naturalistic picture which captured the very essence of Adam at his best.

Not that I took in all the detail but, for me, what really summed the whole picture up, were Adam's eyes, which had a frighteningly forlorn, beseeching look in them. Like a little, lost child.

12

From being busy all the time and out practically every night, I sank into a very dull, lonely life.

'How could Adam have done this to me?' I constantly raved at Mel.

For the first time since I'd known her, Mel offered little consolation, though she listened patiently to my heartbroken ramblings. 'Well, he didn't achieve it single-handed, that's for sure!'

'What's that supposed to mean?'

'I'm sorry,' Mel said, 'but I tried to slow you down at the time. I did warn you to think what you were doing.'

'So, now it's all my fault?'

'No, of course not. Look why don't you at least *talk* to Adam?'

Any sane person, even if they hadn't rushed straight round to see Adam, would have done as she suggested, would have instantly got on the phone and tried to start repairing what little remained of the relationship. But, for me, it would have been far easier to return to Tony and tell him I hadn't meant all the things I'd said than, after all this time, to do so much as approach Adam.

Besides, I wasn't sane, I was very, very angry. Naturally, I'd always blamed Adam for destroying the special something I'd thought we'd had. Now I was furious with myself for allowing him to, yet too proud to *do* anything to correct his stupidity. 'It's up to Adam now. He sent me away, now he'll have to beg to get me back.'

'He tried to, frequently, but you wouldn't talk to him, remember?' Mel pointed out.

'Well, it's different now.'

'But Adam's got no way of knowing that, has he?' Mel's eyes brightened. 'I know, why don't you get your mother to drop some sort of hint while she's round there?'

I shook my head. 'The portrait's finished, she doesn't go any more.'

'What does she think you should do?'

I gave Mel a withering look. 'You know how hands-off my mother is. If I so much as utter the word Adam she says, "I'm sure you know what you're doing."'

'Well, you're going to have to do something sooner or later,' Mel said, 'before you drive us both mad.'

'Oh, why can't I be happy to settle for Tony?' I wailed. 'It would all be so much easier. After all, he's good-looking, kind, understanding and very sexy.'

'Sex can be overvalued,' Mel said knowingly.

'You sound like somebody's mother!' I shrieked at her.

'Well, it can,' she insisted.

'Not when you're not getting any, it can't!' I said with a sigh. I was suffering from withdrawal symptoms, missing greatly the exquisite, toe-curling sensations Tony's gentle, skilful touch had aroused in me. 'Tony's only got two real faults.'

'Which are?' Mel asked as if she could hardly care less.

'The main one is, he just isn't Adam.'

'Barring plastic surgery, not a lot he can do about that,' she yawned. 'And the other?'

'His two favourite topics of conversation were you and cars, in that order! If he wasn't raving on about some purple romper suit you wore for your fourth birthday party, then it was the latest car he was working on in his wretched garage.'

Mel instantly perked up. '*His* garage? You never

mentioned he had his own garage.'

'Under the flat! I thought you knew because you told me about him doing up the E-type.'

'Yes, but I thought that was during his spare time, in some lock-up.'

'Oh, no,' I assured her. 'He gets lots of work because people have discovered how honest and reliable he is. As a matter of fact, he was thinking of expanding and taking on more mechanics.'

'Was he?'

I swear I could hear the whirring of Mel's mental computer as she updated Tony's file. 'But that's all beside the point,' I said, struggling to return to my worries, 'and it certainly doesn't solve my problem.'

'We're the only people who can do that,' Mel said gloomily. 'In the end we've all got to solve our own problems.'

Maybe if I hadn't been so selfishly involved with my own affairs, I might have noticed how miserable she sounded and asked what had led to that piece of homespun philosophy, but I didn't.

To be honest, something was really beginning to bother me. I had no doubts about really loving Adam, but I realised there was one big snag. Just because people are apart that doesn't mean they stop growing and the relationship I'd had with Tony was very physical, full of hugs and real kisses.

Even supposing I got Adam back, how well would I be able to cope again without all that? Would I still be willing to settle for touching palms either side of a sheet of plastic?

At school, Miss Weinstock kept asking how our projects were going.

I always answered, 'Fine.'

But of course it wasn't. I'd hardly opened my folder since

I last saw Adam. With no material from the class visits to fall back on, there was nothing to add. It would probably never be finished.

Then, one day, Miss Weinstock announced, 'I'd like all project folders in for a progress check. It's no use waiting until the last minute to discover you've been heading in the wrong direction.'

I swore I hadn't brought mine with me and promised to bring it in for the next time we met.

What was I going to do now? All my entries were dated. The moment she opened it, Miss Weinstock would know I hadn't touched it for ages.

I considered the idea of telling her I'd given up the project but then I dismissed it. To give up that meant giving up Adam and I really wasn't about to do that, not without a fight.

And that was the reason why, at long last, I convinced myself, still trying to hug the last shreds of my pride around me like an old lady in a tattered shawl. I rang Adam.

Having spent hours plucking up the courage, dialling half the number and replacing the receiver, when I eventually did let it ring there was no reply.

'Typical!' I yelled at the useless instrument. I was the only person who ever rang Adam's personal number, so he must have known it was me, which was why he hadn't bothered to answer! Furious, I stormed round to his house and banged on the front door.

Not surprisingly, Mrs Simmonds wasn't very welcoming. 'Hello, stranger. To what do we owe the honour of this visit?'

I was in no mood for an argument. 'I've come to see Adam.'

'Well, I'm sorry, you can't!'

'Isn't that up to him?' I said rudely, as I pushed past her, heading for the living room.

But the second I opened the door I realised why she'd said what she had. The room was in complete darkness and deadly silent, not even the ever-present hum from his air-supply pump.

Adam wasn't there.

The only remaining sign of him was the portrait, his eyes staring accusingly at me.

'What's happened?' I cried. 'Where's Adam?'

'In hospital.'

The thought instantly flashed into my mind that something dreadful must have happened to him! Why had I been so stubborn and let my stupid pride stop me getting in touch with him? 'Oh, no!' was all I managed to say, before I burst into tears.

All the mess, the frustration, the anger, all of it came out at that moment, in sobs which shuddered through my whole body. Considering how I'd behaved, it would have been perfectly understandable if Mrs Simmonds had ignored my outburst and thrown me out, but she didn't. Instead she said, 'I think you'd better come through to the kitchen and sit down.'

Having put a box of tissues on the table in front of me, she didn't say another word until she'd made us both coffee.

Later, buried in a snowdrift of used Kleenex, I'd calmed down a little, though tears were still trickling down my cheeks and my nose was running. I felt a total wreck. I've always envied girls who can cry and still look pretty. When I'm really upset, I go puffy all round my eyes. Hideous red blotches erupt on my usually pale cheeks and my nose turns into a ginormous, soggy, sore elephant's trunk.

'I don't understand why you're so surprised,' she said. 'Adam wouldn't be in hospital now, if it wasn't for you.'

'You mean, *I've* made him ill?' I felt another monsoon blowing up.

Mrs Simmonds looked puzzled. 'What? Oh, that. Well,

yes, he was very depressed for a while after you stopped coming to see him.'

'Did he tell you why I stopped?'

'No, he didn't, but it didn't surprise me. I thought you'd soon grow tired of the idea, everybody does. Which was why I said from the very beginning, it would be better if you didn't start coming round.'

If Adam hadn't told her what he'd said to me, I thought it was best left alone. 'But if I haven't made him ill, why is he in hospital?'

'After all that fuss about Adam in the papers, they sent a journalist from the *Lancet*.'

'Adam said they were going to.'

'Well, about three weeks ago, the article was published and a Japanese scientist, who's been doing a lot of research on SCID, got in touch with the hospital. He said he had some new ideas and he'd like to examine Adam to see if there was anything he could do to help.'

I couldn't believe it! 'Adam always said they'd find a cure!'

Mrs Simmonds shook her head. 'Not so fast.'

But the slightest hint of a miracle cure had sent my mind racing ahead, to the possibility of Adam being able to walk out of his plastic prison, free after all those years. 'But this could be the break-through we've all been hoping for!'

She smiled at me. 'I know it's the first time this has happened since you knew Adam, but we've been through this scores of times. They think of something new but, when they try it, it fails and we're back to square one. I wouldn't get your hopes up. I won't believe it until I can see the evidence with my own eyes.'

Even though Mrs Simmonds was talking down the idea, I could tell she was still desperately hoping that this time things would turn out differently. She just didn't dare say the words. 'Besides,' she added, 'we won't know anything for some time. He only went in yesterday.'

Kicking myself for not having come sooner, I asked if I could go and see him in hospital, but she shook her head. 'I'm afraid he can't have any visitors. He's in the usual, total isolation room, and they said he must have complete rest while they perform all the tests.'

Remembering what Adam had told me, I said, 'At least you'll get some proper rest while he's away.'

She smiled. 'I suppose so, but it doesn't really matter where he is, I still worry about him.'

'I'm sure you do.'

Mrs Simmonds let out a deep sigh. 'Sometimes I feel guilty for bringing Adam into the world.'

'Guilty?'

'Before he was born, the doctors warned us about the possibility of him having SCID. You see, Adam wasn't our first baby. His sister Sarah was born two years earlier, but it was a difficult birth and she hadn't the strength. She couldn't put up the fight Adam did. Sarah was four months old when she died. A tiny, scrap of a thing, she was. It was only afterwards we found out she'd suffered from SCID and the doctors told us there was more than an even chance any baby we had would suffer from the same problem. Of course, I thought I knew better.'

'You could have been right.'

'The doctors didn't think so. They took no chances. Adam was born by Caesarean. I'd barely seen him and certainly not been allowed to give him a cuddle, before they whisked him off into the isolation room they'd got ready. I've never held Adam in my arms, not without using those wretched rubber gloves.'

I knew only too well how she felt. I was positive that if Adam and I had been able to get together, properly, the question of Tony would never have arisen. 'But I'm sure Adam doesn't blame you for his problems. Mostly, he seems

111

to accept the situation better than the rest of us. Besides, I'm sure he would far rather have been born than not.'

'I wish I could be certain of that.'

Really expressing hopes for Adam and my future together too, I said, 'I'm sure everything's going to turn out all right in the end.'

But Mrs Simmonds preferred to remain pessimistic. 'Like I said, don't hold your breath!'

Having re-established contact, every day, on the way home from school, I made a point of visiting Mrs Simmonds and I was quite surprised to find it wasn't such a chore. Apart from being the only way I could get up-to-date news of Adam, I could feel a common bond beginning to grow between us. I'm sure that was partly because, in spite of the extra rest she was getting, she not only worried about him, but missed him, desperately. But whatever the reason, we got on far better then than we ever had while Adam was around.

During the first week Adam was in hospital, another bombshell burst. Late one night, my extension phone, which I'd plugged in again, in the vain hope that Adam would find a way of calling, at long last rang.

I snatched it up but, when nobody spoke, I dismissed it as either a heavy breather, or a potential burglar casing the joint! Putting on my most grown-up sounding voice, I demanded, 'Who's there?'

I could have sworn I heard smothered sobs and knowing no boys who would ring, let alone who'd cry down the phone, my heart skipped a beat as I thought of Adam. 'Mrs Simmonds, is that you? Has something happened to Adam?'

A small voice, choking with sobs, said, 'No, it's me, Mel.'

I suffered instant pangs of guilt. Mel, who'd been far from her usual breezy self for ages, hadn't been at school that day and I'd fully intended to ring her to find out how she was, but had forgotten. 'Mel, what on earth's the matter?'

The only reply I got was an anguished wail.

'For heaven's sake, Mel, what is it?'

Between sobs, all she managed to get out was, 'It's so awful, I can't tell you!'

'But, Mel, how can I possibly help unless you tell me what's wrong?'

After a very long pause, in a choked whisper, she eventually got out the words, 'I think I'm pregnant.'

I was so stunned, before I could stop myself, I said, 'How did that happen?'

Mel snapped back, 'How do you think? It isn't going to be a virgin birth!'

'Rob?'

'Of course Rob! Who else?'

'What are you going to do?'

'I don't know.'

'Have you told your parents?'

'I'm not positive yet, but my periods are usually so regular and this one's a fortnight late.'

No wonder she'd been off school! 'Does Rob know?'

There was a renewed burst of sobbing. 'Rob doesn't *want* to know!'

'What?'

'When I told him, all he said was, "If you are, you'll have to get rid of it!"'

'Oh, Mel, you poor thing. But I thought everything was so great between you two.'

'So did I.'

'All those promises about helping you to become a model.'

'Oh, that!' Mel said scornfully. 'That was all talk.'

'I wondered why the studio session was so long coming.'

'Oh, we did it!' Mel said bitterly.

'But you said you wanted me to go with you.'

'I did, but Rob didn't and when I arrived, I soon found out why! You remember he was going to borrow all those clothes from designers he knew? Well, there weren't any clothes. Just some disgusting underwear.'

'Oh, Mel! You didn't, did you?'

Mel sounded very uncomfortable. 'I didn't want to, but he went on and on at me. In the end he made it sound so reasonable, I gave in, but it was horrible. I felt cheap and dirty!'

'But if you didn't want to . . .'

'Anne, life's not that simple, when you think you love someone and can trust them.'

Remembering the confused thoughts and emotions I'd experienced with Tony, I was forced to agree.

'But now I think I'm pregnant, the little rat's dumped me!'

'So much for the Porsche,' I said quietly.

'Oh, that's the final straw. He hasn't got a Porsche any more. In fact, he never had. It was rented, to impress people, and now they've taken it back because he couldn't keep up the payments. That's Rob all over! I realise that now; all show and talk! Oh, Anne, I've been such an idiot. What am I going to do?'

'You could get a pregnancy testing kit. You know, one of those DIY jobs.'

'I'd already thought of that, but I keep putting it off. I know it sounds stupid, but at the moment I only *think* I might be pregnant. If I used one, and it proved positive, I'd know for sure and I don't want to know!'

'You'll find out sooner or later anyway, even if you wait nine months!'

'Thanks, that's really cheered me up!'

'But, Mel, you have to know, so that you can decide what you're going to do about having the baby, or not. Your parents will have to be involved in that discussion.'

'I can't tell my father! He'll probably throw me straight out of the house without bothering to open the door!'

'Of course he won't. Anyway, you could always talk to your mother first, see what she thinks.'

'She'll say she always knew something like this would happen. I wish I'd got an understanding mum, like yours.'

'Sometimes it isn't as easy as you think, living here. Mum would probably forget I'd told her, suggest I go on a diet when she eventually noticed I was getting fat and then be amazed when I produced a baby.'

'I can't have a baby!' Mel shrieked at me.

'You'd rather have an abortion?'

'I'd have to, wouldn't I? How could I look after a baby? I haven't even finished school. I've no money and, if I left before A-levels, no qualifications to even try and get a job.'

'All the more reason for talking to your mother. The longer you put it off, the more difficult it'll be to arrange an abortion.'

Mel didn't sound convinced. 'I suppose you're right. Oh, what an awful mess and all because of that ratfink Rob!'

I tried to sound positive. 'Things will work out, you'll see. Better get some sleep and we'll talk tomorrow.'

'Not at school! Don't even hint at it. You know what they're like. Rumours spread quicker than measles round there! The head would know by first break!'

'Okay, take care, and ring me whenever you like.'

'I rang earlier but you weren't in.'

'I went round to see Mrs Simmonds.'

'Any news about Adam?'

'Nothing and even Mrs Simmonds still isn't allowed to

visit him yet. I just wish there was some way of letting Adam know I'm thinking of him. He probably thinks I'm still going out with Tony.'

'Why can't she give him a message?'

'How could I do that without telling her the whole sordid story? I don't want to ruin everything, not now we're getting on so well.'

'Isn't there a phone by his bed?'

'Mrs Simmonds said not.'

'Oh, dear,' Mel sighed, 'we're both in it up to our necks, aren't we? See you tomorrow.'

After I'd said good night, whilst I could understand Mel's reasoning, I couldn't help thinking about her being so certain she wanted an abortion. It seemed so unfair that while Mel would probably have given birth to a perfectly healthy baby, Mrs Simmonds still suffered guilt from having brought Adam into the world.

And yet, suppose Adam had never been born . . .?

13

Mrs Simmonds was bubbling like a volcano about to erupt. 'Mr Kimoto's convinced he's found a way of giving Adam the beginnings of an immune system by introducing into his body some bone-marrow taken from a healthy person. If the transfer worked, Adam's body could slowly build on that until he had the same amount of resistance as everyone else.'

After the endless, empty days of waiting (not to mention two more days of agonising with Mel over when/if she should talk to her mother) it was wonderful to have some really good news.

'Would anybody's bone-marrow do? He's welcome to some of mine. My bones are my strongest point. Mel swears a single jab from my elbow could pierce a truck tyre.'

'Mr Kimoto said, to be successful, the marrow has to genetically match Adam's as closely as possible. Close relatives are most likely. They find out by testing a blood sample and tomorrow I'm going with his father to have ours done.'

'Will you see Adam?'

Mrs Simmonds nodded. 'They said we might be allowed in, just for a few minutes. Is there any message you'd like me to give him?'

Obviously yes, but what? What I *most* wanted to say wasn't the kind of thing you could pass on through somebody's mother, even mine! 'Tell him, I've been thinking about him, a lot, while he's been away and I've *really* missed him.'

'Yes, I will,' she promised.

Then Mrs Simmonds surprised me. She'd always seemed to back away from any kind of physical contact. She'd sooner risk dropping the mug than let my hand accidentally touch hers as she passed me a coffee. Mum had tried to shake hands with her, when they first met, but Mrs Simmonds had pretended not to notice. Maybe it was some kind of mental block, all part of not being allowed to touch Adam. So it came as quite a shock, when she suddenly laid her hand on mine and said, 'Anne, you've been a great comfort to me while Adam's been in hospital. I know how grumpy I can be when he is around but, without him, everywhere seems so empty. I don't know how I'd have got through these last few days without you to talk to.'

As she spoke, I realised how close we'd become, but all I could say in reply was, 'I hope your tests work out.'

But they didn't. Mrs Simmonds told me they weren't even close. 'Apparently it's not unusual for parents to be a mis-match.' Although it was obvious she was disappointed, she hadn't given up hope. 'We have to get all the uncles, aunts and cousins tested next.'

They proved fruitless too.

By then, Mrs Simmonds was still quite calm, but I was getting frantic. Days were slipping by and I still hadn't been allowed anywhere near Adam. The buoyancy brought about by the hope of this new treatment was continually escaping, like air from a tyre with a slow puncture. 'Is that it then? Will they give up?'

'Oh, no. It's just that Adam happens to be a rare type and difficult to match, but there's a bank of donors who are willing to give marrow and the doctors will work their way through those next.'

'But what if none of those match either?' I watched Mrs Simmonds' face crumple. I wished I hadn't asked and then tried to counter it with a suggestion. 'Why don't I take the test?'

'Everyone's welcome to try,' she said doubtfully. 'Even if Adam can't use your bone-marrow, maybe somebody else could.'

Although the Blood Transfusion Service regularly visited our area, until that moment I'd always dismissed them as Werewolves-on-Wheels. The thought of accidentally cutting myself with a knife froze my stomach with horror, so the idea of voluntarily allowing someone to let my blood flow freely seemed positively ghoulish. But if it might help Adam, get me into the same building and, perhaps, even to see him for a few moments, offering myself up seemed a small sacrifice to make! Ugh!

Knowing that telling anyone would only make them tease me, I'd secretly arranged to have the test done after school one afternoon. All that day, unable to concentrate, I suffered from a horrendous repeated image from *Nightmare on Elm Street*, the scene where geysers of blood spurt up and hit the walls and ceiling.

By lunch-time I thought I'd finally flipped when, having escaped into the cloakroom, I found dark drops of blood, congealing all over the chipped, white basins. At the time, the real explanation, Josie having another nosebleed, sounded less probable than a visitation from Lady Macbeth's ghost.

So you'll understand that by the time I was walking down the High Street, on my way to the hospital, I was in a highly nervous condition. This explains why, when a strange car suddenly halted right beside me with a violent squeal of brakes, I almost passed out.

Scraping myself up off the pavement, I heard a familiar voice asking, 'What's up with you?'

'Tony, you scared me half to death.'

'Where are you going?'

'The hospital.'

'Best place, by the look of you. You're white as a sheet.'

'Tony, I'm deeply offended that you've already forgotten my natural skin tone,' I said with a laugh. 'Actually, there's nothing wrong with me, I'm going to give a blood sample.'

'You don't look as if you've got much to spare!' Tony said with a grin. 'Hop in! I'm taking this car on a test drive for its MOT certificate, so I might as well make myself useful and run you up there.'

After all we'd been through together, and the things we hadn't, I felt quite awkward about being alone with him again in the confined space of a car, but time was short, so I gratefully accepted the offer.

Just in case Tony had other ideas, I quickly explained that Adam's illness was the reason behind the blood test. 'To see if my bone-marrow could be used to help him.'

Judging by his rather glum, 'I see,' I could tell Tony was disappointed Adam and I were back together. That's all he knew! Before he could ask any questions, I got mine in first. 'Have you rung Mel yet?'

'Don't be silly!' Tony said, scornfully. 'Mel never wants to talk to me.'

'That may have changed. She's feeling a bit down. This could be exactly the right moment to give her a ring.'

'Are you serious?'

'Tony, what have you got to lose? Go on, give it a go!'

Although the Head Vampire, a nurse with a broad smile, was very pleasant and comforting, I still had difficulty convincing myself the flecks on her teeth were really lipstick and not blood.

I nervously uttered my worst fear. 'I hope you know when to stop.'

'We only need a smear,' she assured me, dabbing my arm with cotton-wool.

I pretended to count the ceiling tiles. 'But what if, once it's started, my blood won't stop flowing? I don't want to leave here looking like an empty sausage skin!'

The Head Vampire had the nerve to laugh! 'I think, if you were a haemophiliac, you'd know by now.'

Not for nothing was I born with a broad yellow streak down my back. At the last moment I whimpered, 'Will it hurt?'

'Obviously not, I've just done it.'

Stupidly, I turned, saw a microscopic blob of my blood on a glass slide and felt distinctly queasy.

'You aren't going to faint on me, are you?' she asked.

'Definitely not,' I lied and struggling to get my mind off the subject, asked, 'Is there any chance of seeing Adam while I'm here?'

Her thirst sated, the Head Vampire became all business-like and brisk. 'You'll have to ask at Reception.'

I'd been so busy thinking of Adam, I hadn't realised how near Christmas was until, as I walked back into Reception, I almost bumped into two men in brown jackets who were struggling with an enormous tree.

Not that there was any mistletoe dangling over the Robot Woman who guarded this particular hospital. She was backed up by a formidable computer which was specifically programmed to deal with obstinate troublemakers like me. For starters, both flatly denied all knowledge of anyone by the name of Kimoto. When I pointed out that Mr Kimoto was helping to treat Adam Simmonds, Robot Woman tested the keyboard to destruction by punching in his name.

For a second, the computer appeared about to relent, but then Robot Woman's eyes lit up with a metallic gleam as she read from the screen: 'Visitors only permitted with prior permission from Mr Jackman.'

Determined not to give up, I insisted, 'Then, I'd like to ask Mr Jackman for permission.'

Robot Woman's fuses suffered overload. 'You can't talk to a specialist without an appointment.'

'Fine,' I said, trying out my most bewitching smile. 'I'd like to make an appointment to see Mr Jackman. Today, preferably now.'

Robot Woman's lips compressed heavily around her Input Data Acceptance Port as she keyed in his details and the screen revealed his schedule in glorious livid colour. 'Mr Jackman's consultation rota,' she announced, 'is divided into quarter-hour segments and has no vacancies for today.'

Robot Woman's eyes moved to the next victim in the short queue which was starting to form behind me, but I wasn't going to be passed over. In a voice of Sticky-Sweet-Reason I said, 'I won't need a quarter-hour segment. I only want to ask him a simple question with a yes/no answer, which'll take ten seconds, tops. What's he doing now?'

Her eyes swivelled off the person behind me and back to the screen. 'Finishing afternoon ward rounds,' she hissed.

'Well, maybe he finished early. Why don't you ring him, find out and if so, ask if he'll spare me a second?'

Had I raised my voice, or looked remotely annoyed, Robot Woman would have instantly self-destructed all over me. Faced by me at my most angelic and surrounded by potential allies, she gave in, growling, as she stabbed the telephone key pad, 'This is highly irregular!'

What she said to Mr Jackman I couldn't tell. Having penetrated the inner sanctum, her voice faded to a hushed whisper, suitable for a Robot Woman when addressing a higher life form. Whatever was said, she reeked her vengeance on the phone by trying to destroy it with the handset and snapped at me, 'Room 237.'

As I searched the labyrinth for Room 237, I knew my reserves of courage had been extracted by Robot Woman. I wished I'd brought a ball of wool with me, that way I could have left a trail behind me for when Mr Jackman angrily chased me out of the building. But for one of the most respected specialists in his field, Mr Jackman turned out to be an absolute doll!

'Come in,' he said in response to my knock and immediately invited me to sit down.

A tiny, middle-aged man with a pasty complexion and grey, wavy hair, his white coat hung open over a grey, chalk-striped suit. At first glance, he appeared to be in the slow, evolutionary process of fading to nothing but, if he had, I'm convinced his intensely blue eyes would have remained, hanging in the air, like the disembodied parts of the Cheshire Cat. Their impish twinkle gave the impression that, far from being important, he saw himself as an imposter, who only wore the stethoscope dangling over his waistcoat as a mock chain of office.

'You must be rather special,' he said quietly.

'Me? Why?'

'Few evade the clutches of Spiderwoman! What can I do for you that's so important?'

'My name is Anne. I came in for a blood test, to see if my bone-marrow would be suitable for Adam Simmonds. While I'm here, I wondered if I could see him, just for a minute.'

'Ah!' His eyes glittered like gems swept by lasers. 'Adam is a particular friend of yours?'

'Yes, he is,' I said cautiously, but there was something about Mr Jackman which encouraged honesty. 'Because of a . . . misunderstanding . . . we hadn't spoken for several weeks before he came into hospital. Of course, I sent a message with his mother but . . .'

'But that isn't the same thing as talking face to face.' Mr Jackman examined me thoughtfully, as if I'd been an unusual sample which had been delivered to his office.

Elbows widely spaced on the desk, he joined together his paper-white, neatly manicured, fingers precisely at their tips and gazed over them at me. Had he specialised in bones, or even plastic surgery, I could have understood his interest!

Finally he said, 'What I need to know is, are you going to be good for my patient?'

I struggled to rid myself of the honesty, but failed. 'I don't know. We kind of fell out but, like I said, it was all a misunderstanding and I want to make it up to him.'

'You see,' Mr Jackman tipped his head to one side to get a different view of me, like a bird watching a particularly juicy worm, 'Adam and I have been through a lifetime together. He is a very special patient and these are trying times for him. The suggestion Mr Kimoto's come up with has got Adam really on the boil. It's understandable, but when we find a donor and try the experiment, then it's imperative that Adam should be at his strongest. There'll be an enormous strain placed on all of Adam's mental and physical resources. You understand?' I nodded. 'The waiting and the excitement are already causing him to lose sleep.'

'Oh, dear.'

'And whilst you may be looking forward to seeing Adam, the same might not be true for him. You may cause him further distress.'

I could sense myself being metaphorically eased towards the exit. 'But suppose,' I said hastily, 'what happened is bothering Adam, as much as it is me? If I could clear that up, it would be one thing less for him to worry about.'

The pause, while he considered this, seemed endless, but eventually Mr Jackman broke it. 'Let's find out. Come on!'

Leaping out from behind his desk, he shot out of the room and disappeared down the corridor. Far from being the Cheshire Cat, he was really the White Rabbit, shooting along his burrow. As nurses scattered to either side of him, and I ran to catch up, I wouldn't have been remotely surprised to hear him shout, 'I'm late! I'm late!'

He pulled up equally abruptly and I almost flattened him. 'Sorry!' he apologised. 'When God gave us the power to stop quickly, he ought to have given us brake-lights too. This is Adam's room. Just to be on the safe side, I'm going in first, to tell him you're here. I'd rather he didn't die of shock!'

Mr Jackman left me looking longingly at the door. Like all the others in the corridor, it was a perfectly plain, green door, except the card in the brass frame bore Adam's name and beneath, in plastic letters, was the slightly ominous inscription, Isolation Room.

While I waited, a jumble of thoughts tumble-dried in my mind. Perhaps Adam was best left alone and maybe I should get out before I did any more damage, that was countered by the idea that, after all this, Adam might refuse to see me. The temptation not to wait for his decision and to burst in, was tremendous, but I knew I had to resist it.

Craziest of all thoughts, I suddenly wished I'd brought him a present, a box of sweets, or something. Then I remembered he was still in isolation and wouldn't be allowed to eat them. But at least I could have brought him something to look at, like a pot plant. Knowing how he probably felt about me, an ideal reminder might have been a nice deadly nightshade, or a Venus's fly-trap.

After an eternity, Mr Jackman, swathed in a surgeon's robe, emerged wreathed in smiles. 'Guess who's the most popular doctor in the building?'

'Adam wants to see me?'

'More than that! When I told him you were here, he threatened to come out and get you, if I didn't send you in immediately.'

'Thanks,' I said and was about to go through the door when his hand brushed my arm.

'Ten minutes, no more, I mean it!' The way his eyes twinkled, I felt my worst punishment would be being beaten about the ears with a feather-duster, until he added, 'After that I'll send Spiderwoman in to get you!'

I passed through the door, expecting to see Adam, but instead found myself in a small ante-room. From a sealed plastic sack, Mr Jackman produced a set of sterile overalls, similar to his, complete with cloth overshoes, gloves and a mask. 'Slip these on over your clothes, we're taking no chances.'

I felt I was dressed like a cross between a masked raider and a zombie sent to explore an area of nuclear devastation.

As I opened the inner door, even through my mask, I was hit by a wave of chilled air, so heavily laced with antiseptic it was like walking through liquid glass.

Adam sat cross-legged in the middle of the bed, dressed in a pair of deep blue, tracksuit-style, pyjamas.

Just as at home, his whole bed and bedside cupboard were cocooned in plastic sheeting. Apart from a couple of white plastic chairs, the air pump, some transparent tubing and a chrome trolley of medical equipment, the rest of the windowless room was bare. There was nothing which might hold the slightest particle of dirt and therefore germs.

Although there was a small TV at the end of the bed, the general air of sterile bleakness was emphasised by the fluorescent lights and my echoing footsteps, as I crossed the miles of tiled floor to reach Adam.

'Hi!' I said, not realising that here there was no amplifier to pick up my voice.

When he called back, 'Speak up, I can't hear you,' his words were muffled.

I waved to make my meaning clear and called out, 'Hi,' again.

'Hi, yourself! You shouldn't have bothered to dress up specially just for me!'

The trouble was, by the time I'd twice asked him to repeat what he'd said, his remark had lost most of its humour.

I'd always known we might have trouble talking to each other again after such a long time, but with me wearing a mask and Adam sounding as if he was underwater, it was proving next to impossible. To make matters worse, as I tried desperately to get my next point across, 'I wanted to tell you, I'm sorry for walking out on you,' Adam kept turning away.

'Walking . . . what?' he asked, but before I could repeat it, he was gone again.

'Adam, for heaven's sake, sit still,' I shouted at him and slapped the plastic sheet in fury. But he was waving a phone at me.

I couldn't believe it! Mr Jackman had only allowed us ten measly minutes together. Why on earth was Adam wasting them, making a phone call?

With much pointing and waving, Adam finally made me understand there was a similar one on my side. When I picked it up, we could hear each other perfectly!

'I thought you hadn't got a phone.'

'It's only an intercom, like they have in American jails, so that I can talk to visitors. I can't dial out or take calls. Now, what was that bit about walking?' he asked.

Being made to repeat it was even worse than making Adam repeat his feeble joke. 'I said, I was sorry I'd walked out on you.'

'Forget it! It's me who should be sorry,' Adam said. 'It

was all my fault. I made you do it.'

'But I knew it was a daft idea and I shouldn't have let you make me.' As I went on, I looked away from him. Without being able to see his reaction, it felt easier, more anonymous. Just like the old days of chatting on the phone at home. 'When it first started, I really didn't want to go out with Tony. I only did it to teach you a lesson.'

There was a pause before Adam asked unsteadily, 'Did you enjoy it?'

'Going out with him? Yes, it was okay, but I would far rather have been with you.'

'Was that why you kept going out with him for so long?'

Glancing sideways, I realised Adam had never taken his eyes off me. I wriggled uncomfortably as I answered. 'Well, he's a nice guy. It was fun, just like you'd said it would be. Trouble was, we began to get more and more involved with each other.'

The next pause was very long, before Adam asked in a hoarse whisper, 'How *involved*?'

I felt myself starting to blush as I tried to reassure him. 'Oh, nothing happened.'

'What sort of "nothing"?'

'We just kissed and stuff.'

'Stuff?'

'Adam, stop repeating everything I say!'

'Okay. I'll ask a proper question. Was this Tony a good kisser?'

I felt my fingernails biting into my palms as my fists clenched in a confused cocktail of guilt, anger and frustration, which had been brewing for weeks. 'Yes, he was, if you must know. He was very good!' Then the potent mixture began to well up inside me and I faced Adam, shouting into the phone, 'Listen, Adam! I'd never have gone out with him in the first place, if you hadn't forced me into it.'

Adam seemed unmoved. In spite of the intimate questions he was asking, he just sat there, staring at me, as if he were quizzing a total stranger. Very quietly, he went for the $64,000 question. 'Did you make love together?'

That did it!

I screamed at Adam, 'I wanted to, don't think I didn't, but when it came to the point, I couldn't.'

'Couldn't?' Adam looked very pale. 'What do you mean, couldn't?'

'I couldn't because of you, Adam, damn you! All the time I kept thinking of you, wishing they were your hands touching me, not Tony's. So, in the end, I bloody well couldn't do it!'

When I next glanced at Adam, I saw that his eyes were tightly closed and there was a single tear trickling down his right cheek.

At first his lips moved, but no sound came out. Then, very slowly, in a monotone, he managed the words. 'You've no idea what a relief that is. All this time, I've been going crazy with jealousy. I know I've been totally stupid.'

'You can say that again!' I growled.

'Anne, I love you more than anyone else in the whole world and I didn't mean to do anything to hurt you. I know now how crazy it was, but I just wasn't thinking straight. I'd got so used to asking you to try things for me, at the time it seemed just . . . just like one more thing.'

'That wasn't what you said at the time.'

'I know, I lied. But worse still, it didn't strike me until you'd gone, what a mad, useless idea it was. You going out, doing things and then coming back to tell me how they felt was no substitute for the real thing. All you could tell me was how *you* felt, but I was no wiser. It didn't get me a micro-spec closer to knowing how *I* would feel if I'd done the things myself.'

'Sometimes I felt like a rat in a laboratory experiment.

You know, "Let's see what happens if we put some of this in its eye! Oh, dear, it's gone blind, I thought it might."'

'I'm sorry. It's just that, stuck in here, there are so many things I don't know and I thought it was a way of . . .' Adam's voice trailed off for a moment.

'Well,' I said, 'maybe you'll be coming out of there soon and we can try things together.'

For the first time since I'd entered his room, a glimmer of a smile lit Adam's face before he said, 'I'll never forget all those terrible weeks, when I wasn't able to see you and talk to you. I learned something about feelings and emotions and I know, whatever happens, I never want to run the risk of losing you again.'

Instinctively, my hand went out towards Adam. It met the plastic barrier but, from the other side, his joined mine and, to my great relief, I felt the old, familiar, comforting tingle, as if our spirits mingled. And yet, at the same time, I couldn't help feeling impatient for the day when that last barrier would finally be removed, when, hopefully, I wouldn't be dressed like the star of *The Curse of the Mummy*.

'Did you know Winston Churchill had a butterfly farm?'

'What?'

'Once, during a garden party, he released six hundred specially bred peacock butterflies.'

'What a wonderful thing to do!'

'Was it?'

I was startled to see that Adam's expression had changed completely. From being all smiles, he suddenly looked angry, almost as if he was accusing me of something. 'Well, of course it was. Why shouldn't they have their freedom?'

'Anne, it's not that simple!' He almost spat the words at me. 'Think about it for a minute. All those butterflies had been living in the safety of their cage. Nothing to harm them, not even the weather and all they could eat, without even having to hunt for it.'

I was beginning to see where this conversation was leading. 'Even so,' I said, 'surely it was better they had their freedom and took their chances in the outside world?'

'Oh, it was a grand gesture,' Adam said contemptuously. 'I'm sure his guests were very impressed, but how long do you suppose they'd last out there?'

'I don't know.'

'Protected, a pair of butterflies could produce three million other butterflies in a single season. But in the wild they're lucky if they create just two more. The rest get killed one way or another. Either by being sprayed with insecticide, or from just a sudden change in the weather. Most of the eggs laid never get beyond the caterpillar stage and most of those that do get eaten by birds.'

I chose my words carefully. 'So what you're saying is, Winston Churchill ought to have left them in their cages?'

'At least they were safe.'

'True. But what about all the things they'd never experience? The feel of the sun, the wind . . .'

'Being eaten?'

'Or maybe,' I said firmly, 'the excitement of being chased by some big bird, but escaping to live another day. Surely it's better to take the risk?'

I jumped as Adam thumped the bedside table with his fist. 'That's what I don't know!'

'You're frightened of coming out?' I asked quietly.

'Of course not!' he snapped. 'It's what I've always wanted, dreamed about.'

'But now it's become a real possibility, you're not so sure?'

'*Anne*, I am frightened,' he admitted. 'All my life I've been safe in here, almost nothing could harm me.

Sometimes out there seems so big. Remember, you're talking to somebody who's never walked round the outside of his own house. I'm not sure I'll be able to cope.'

'Of course you will.'

'I've read about people who've been released from prison after a long sentence and who ought to be happy to be free but, far from enjoying it, they can't wait to get back inside.'

'In your case, there's one big difference. I'll be out here waiting for you.'

Suddenly he relaxed. All the anger and fear drained out of him and he gave me one of his lopsided smiles, but there was an evil look in his eyes as he said, 'Trust you to think of the one thing that would put me off the whole idea!'

14

Our English teacher is always telling us two negatives make a positive, as in: I don't not want to go, but I was soon to learn that this isn't always a rule of life.

IR1 was the relieved, plate-speak message Mel slipped to me during science.

The moment we were alone I grabbed her. 'It was all a false alarm, you're not pregnant after all?' Mel didn't answer, merely shook her head. 'What a relief.'

'In some ways, yes,' Mel agreed, but she didn't sound very pleased.

'At least you can get on with your life again.'

She pulled a long face. 'What life?'

'Oh, come on, Mel! There are plenty of men on your list without Rob.'

'And how will I ever be able to trust one again, after the way he's behaved? Apart from running out on me when I most needed him to stand by me, there were all those lies he told about his job and his car. The latest news is, he says he's going to sell those sick pictures he took of me to a magazine.'

'The underwear stuff? Can he do that without your permission?'

'Apparently he can. You know Jodie's father's a journalist? Well, he says that if I'd paid for the session, the copyright of the photographs would be mine, then I'd have to sign a form, called a release, before they could be used. But, because I didn't pay, Rob is free to do anything he likes with them. The rat!'

'Oh, Mel! Even so, all men aren't like Rob.'

'Name one.'

'Adam.'

'Look what he did to you!'

'That's all sorted now. And there's Tony.'

'Oh, I forgot to mention, he rang me the other night.'

I never believed he'd actually do it! 'Oh, really?' I said innocently. 'What did he want?'

'Don't know. He mumbled something about, would I like to go round to his garage some time and have a look at the cars he's working on.'

'Are you going to?'

'Are you serious? Why would I want to crawl around a load of dirty old bangers?'

'Like you once said to me, have you got any better offers at the moment?'

'I think I'll steer clear of cars for a while.'

'But you've still got your project to finish.'

'Maybe I'll start over again and do something completely different . . .'

'But, Mel, there isn't time to start a new one.'

'Mmm. Well, I'll think about it.'

There was nothing positive about the negative result of my blood test either.

Because of an Oriental proverb I'd picked up, I passionately wanted to be the one to help Adam. It says, if you save someone's life, to repay the debt, that person becomes yours for ever. The idea appealed, not because I'm power crazy, but romantically.

Besides, the idea that a tiny part of me could be living and growing inside Adam seemed so wonderful, especially if it would help him resist infection so that he could enjoy a normal life.

Not surprisingly, far from a perfect match, we turned out to be genetic opposites. As Mr Jackman put it, during one of my visits to Adam, 'To be any further apart, one of you would need to have come from a different planet!'

Adam laughed. 'That might explain why I often feel I've spent my life shut up in a spaceship.'

Disappointed as I was, my concern was still for Adam. As we walked down the corridor to Mr Jackman's office, I asked, 'Now what?'.

'Mr Kimoto has been going through the bone-marrow bank,' Mr Jackman said, 'and we've found a boy we think might do.'

For some ridiculous reason, I was really relieved that if it wasn't my bone-marrow going into Adam, at least it wasn't another girl's. But Mr Jackman was usually so up-beat, it was easy to detect the uncertainty in his voice. 'Might do?' I said, raising my eyebrows.

Mr Kimoto, who, on the rare occasions he appeared, always stood respectfully, two paces behind Mr Jackman, behaving like his shadow, said in a low voice which sounded like gravel being crushed, 'It is the nearest we can get. Adam is a very rare type.'

'I'd agree with that!' I said, trying to sound cheerful. 'But isn't this whole experiment very risky?'

Mr Kimoto's nod was almost a bow. 'Yes, of course there are risks, but Adam is growing older and the need greater.'

Mr Jackman slipped an arm around my shoulder. 'So far we've been able to protect Adam from the dangers of the outside world. When he was a baby, that was quite simple. But the older he gets, the more strain he puts on what little immune system he has. It would only take something quite small to upset that very delicate balance. I've always worried that something as harmless as an influenza germ, which wouldn't necessarily harm you or me, might somehow evade our system of control and attack Adam.

135

The result could be fatal.'

Mr Kimoto added, 'In the same way that we have often infected isolated people, like Eskimos and American Indians, who had no immunity to our diseases.'

'Apart from anything else,' Mr Jackman said, 'we have to take into account the quality of Adam's current life style. How much longer can we expect a growing boy to exist in total physical isolation? What kind of future does that hold for him? Now Mr Kimoto has come up with the most likely solution. We've carefully examined all the angles and we believe there's a reasonable possibility of success. I think, for Adam's sake, we have no choice but to try it.'

I could hardly persuade myself to utter the words. 'What are the chances of success?'

'I'll be honest with you,' Mr Jackman said, 'about fifty-fifty. But that's far better than doing nothing and allowing a dreadful natural accident to occur, for which we would have no cure.'

I didn't know what to think. Either way, there seemed the awful possibility of losing Adam for ever. At least, if what Mr Kimoto believed turned out to be true, there was the chance of a miracle. Adam had the chance of something more like real life. 'What does Mrs Simmonds think?'

'Like you, she was concerned, but she's agreed to the operation.'

'And Adam? Have you told him what's involved?'

'Everything and he wants it too.'

I couldn't help feeling very frightened. 'I don't want to sound rude,' I said carefully, 'but, Mr Kimoto, you're a scientist, not a doctor. Isn't there a danger of you thinking of Adam as just another laboratory experiment?'

A very gentle smile bathed Mr Kimoto's face. 'Let me tell you something about myself. Not all Japanese are rich. My own family were very poor. I was their only child and they scraped and saved, in the hope that, one day, I would not have the hard life they had suffered, but go to university. In August of 1945, it happened they sent me to Tokyo for a holiday with my uncle. While I was there my parents were amongst millions who were killed. In many ways they were the lucky ones. Some who survived have lived to regret it. You see, my home town was Hiroshima. I assure you, I have the utmost respect for the value of human life.'

'I'm sorry,' I said, feeling very ashamed.

'Oh, please!' Mr Kimoto said, with a real, low bow.

'Besides,' Mr Jackman added, 'after all the years of protecting Adam, struggling to sustain his life, do you really imagine I would permit an unwarranted chance to be taken now?'

'I don't know what to say,' I whispered down the hospital's bedside phone to Adam. It was the night before the operation was to be performed. Mrs Simmonds, having tactfully left us alone, was waiting for me outside.

'How about, "See you tomorrow"?'

'Aren't you frightened any more?'

'Not really, just excited. I can't stop thinking of all the possibilities if this works. It'll be like being reborn. After all this time, I'll finally be able to leave the womb!'

Trust Adam! Here was I fearing the worst, when it wasn't even happening to me. 'Yes, of course, you're right.'

'Don't worry,' Adam said, making it all sound so simple, 'everything's going okay. Cheer up! Remember what happened when a female skeleton got engaged to a male skeleton and then discovered he'd got a wooden leg.'

'All right,' I groaned, 'what did happen?'

'She broke it off and then told him to hop it!'

'That's sick!'

'I know,' Adam admitted gleefully, 'but at least for a couple of seconds, it stopped you looking so worried. You'd better go, before Mum comes and drags you out. Give us a kiss!'

We touched palms for a long time, neither wanting to be the first to move away. 'Just think,' Adam smiled, 'in a couple of days, there could be the real thing!'

Although I'd always loved Christmas, that evening, as I walked through Reception, I couldn't help feeling how garish the tinsel decorations and twinkling tree lights looked.

Next day, knowing I wouldn't be able to concentrate, Mum agreed I needn't go to school. It was one of those astonishing winter days. The overnight frost heavily coated the bare twigs of the trees like white velvet on deers' antlers. Above them, the sun shone brilliantly out of a totally clear blue sky. Although it was impossible to imagine anything in the world could go wrong on such a day, I was so nervous, I gave up trying to write Christmas cards and went on an eating jag instead. I virtually opened the fridge door, pulled up a chair and devoured the contents.

Around midday, I was hunting the corners of a plastic container, seeking out the last remaining drops left from a litre of toffee ice cream, when the doorbell rang. A menacing Hell's Angel dressed in red leathers, his face obscured by a smoked visor, stood on the doorstep like a visitor from outer space. He was busy shouting unintelligibly into his CB. The words were being chewed up by the helmet's mouthpiece and the return message, having forced its way through a barrage of static, was no clearer, but he seemed satisfied and offered me the cardboard box he was clutching. 'Oteir,' he announced.

I was beginning to think it was some deficiency in me that constantly attracted men with severe communication difficulties. 'Pardon?'

'OTEIR,' he shouted.

We could have spent the rest of the day shouting at each other, if his heavily gauntleted hand hadn't suddenly pointed towards the logo, printed in blue on the box, and beneath it their title, the Hot Air Message Company.

'Thanks,' I said, trying to take the box which he refused to release.

'Sighnear,' he said.

I signed the clipboard he was waving at me and rushed back into the house. The second I opened the box flaps, up popped a shiny red, metallic, gas-filled balloon, which floated straight up to the ceiling.

It had a jolly kind of face printed on it in black. Attached to its long tail was a card, bearing the typed message: 'The balloon's finally gone up! Here's hoping we can soon burst my bubble. All of my love, Adam.'

The afternoon sun had long since faded, giving way again to the iron grip of frost, before Mum returned from work.

'How much longer do I have to wait?' I demanded.

'Not too long, I hope,' she said, examining the empty refrigerator. 'There's only half a loaf and some mouldy cheese left in the house. Hasn't Mrs Simmonds rung?'

'I rang Mr Simmonds and he says she's still at the hospital. Do you think something's gone wrong?'

'I'm sure it hasn't.'

'It's not as if it's a major operation. He only needed a local anesthetic.'

'You'll just have to try and be patient a little longer.'

Easy for her to say! At times like this, Mum's therapy was to drift off into the security of her own private world and paint.

By the time the doorbell rang again, I'd polished off the rest of the loaf, was contemplating the mouldy cheese, and was really worried that the white rug, decorated with leaves and succulent fruit, was starting to look quite edible!

I threw open the front door, expecting to find Mrs Simmonds and was amazed to see Mel, though not the Mel I knew and loved. This one had an old parka thrown over an old T-shirt and jeans, all covered in grime. 'Have you been in an accident?'

Mel sighed with contentment as she brushed past me. 'I've had the most astonishing time.'

'You look as if you'd struck oil.'

'Tony let me help him change the timing chain on a diesel.'

'Don't tell me, after all these years, you've actually discovered what's under the bonnet of a car?'

Mel ignored me. 'It was so fabulous and there's this fantastic, old, twin-carb Triumph we're going to strip down tomorrow.'

'What's a twin-carb Triumph?' I asked in all ignorance.

'You mean you don't know?' Mel looked aghast when I shook my head. 'All the time you spent going out with Tony and you didn't learn anything?'

'Oh, I learned quite a lot, just nothing to do with cars.'

'What a wasted opportunity!'

I still couldn't believe the grubby individual talking to me was Mel. This *was* Mel, who wouldn't use a paperclip in case she chipped her nail varnish, who slid her hands into rubber gloves full of honey and lemon gunge for the good of her cuticles. This was the same girl who, to maintain her flawless complexion, was prepared to lie completely still, for hours on end, with the entire contents of a salad sandwich on her face!

'Mel, are you really serious?'

But she didn't hear a word.

'Anne, I never thought it could be so fascinating. For years I've admired the purr of a well-tuned engine, the roar of an exhaust, the thrust of high-speed acceleration, but I never knew how much work went into making all that happen. Just in one evening Tony's already taught me how to listen properly to tappets.'

True love knows no limits! Fortunately I was rescued by the telephone. It was Mrs Simmonds. 'Anne, I'm sorry to ring so late.'

'It doesn't matter. What's been going on? How's Adam? I've been worried sick.'

'He's fine. I'm sorry, I meant to ring earlier, but somehow I was frightened to leave him.'

'You're sure he's all right?'

'Very tired, mostly from the excitement, but apart from that he's perfectly okay. Mr Jackman and Mr Kimoto are very pleased with him. Adam was ever so good about the op. You'll never believe it, he helped them perform part of it. Sticking these huge needles in himself and things. I couldn't have done it, but he said it didn't bother him a bit!'

'You sound exhausted, Mrs Simmonds.'

'To tell the truth, I'm worn out. With all the waiting more than anything else.'

'You should have an early night.'

'I'm going to have a nice cup of tea and then I'm off to bed, but I couldn't go until I'd rung you.'

'Thank you, that's very kind. I've been worrying all day. Can I go and see Adam tomorrow?'

'Not tomorrow. Mr Jackman said Adam ought to have a complete rest and nobody should go tomorrow, but the day after.'

That night as I lay in bed with the lights out and the curtains open, I couldn't help noticing the contrast between the cold, steely eye of the full moon and the warm red glow of Adam's balloon, as it confidently bobbed about my ceiling.

• • •

Stupidly, I'd expected, the next time I went to see Adam, he would already have emerged from his plastic tent, like a butterfly from its cocoon, but real life doesn't work out that way. In fact, nothing changed for a week, though Adam was always pleased to see me and he seemed bright enough. Apart from a dressing on his arm, where they'd injected the bone-marrow into his bloodstream, there was nothing to see.

By the second weekend I was growing impatient. 'When are they going to get rid of all this plastic stuff?'

'Keep your hair on!' Adam said calmly. 'They won't do anything drastic until they're certain it's safe. They keep testing me every day.'

'Tests! How much longer?'

'Anne, I've been waiting sixteen years for this, a few more days won't matter.'

'Yes, I'm sorry, I don't have your patience.'

'It sort of goes with the territory,' Adam said apologetically. 'I was never given the choice.'

'I'm only impatient because I can't wait to get my hands on you!'

Adam laughed. 'Me too! But in a funny kind of way, after all this time, I can't really believe it's finally going to happen.'

But it did, though not quite in the way we expected.

15

Alarm bells first rang when Adam developed a fever and began to have difficulty keeping down food.

At first Mr Jackman, though watching everything carefully, calmly dismissed the signs. 'I'm certain this has nothing to do with rejecting the bone-marrow. It must be a secondary complication. Adam's probably eaten something which has disagreed with him. We've had similar problems in the past, when a relatively harmless bug manages to nip through the food purification process.'

But the symptoms persisted, treatments used didn't appear to help and Adam developed chronic diarrhoea.

Mr Jackman looked more worried and Mr Kimoto spent all his time in the lab, peering into his microscope, trying to identify the exact strain of the germ that was making Adam ill.

My visits were becoming less frequent. Not because I wasn't as eager to see Adam, but because Mrs Simmonds kept ringing, usually just as I was about to leave for the hospital, to put me off.

'Adam's very tired today,' she would say. 'Why don't you leave it until the weekend?'

However, when the weekend arrived, she always found another reason why I should stay away. 'Mr Jackman says Adam needs total rest.'

But in spite of that, Adam being a special patient without set visiting hours, Mrs Simmonds was hardly away from his bedside.

In some ways this was understandable. After all, she *was* his mother, but the atmosphere between us was worsening, more like the crusty days when we first met, and I was getting paranoid about the way she was deliberately easing me out. If things went on that way, she would soon have Adam completely to herself.

But I kept those feelings to myself. Adam had enough problems without being bothered by my paranoia. He was so pleased to see me when I did manage to slip in. He didn't seem to notice how rare these visits were becoming or that it needed tyre-levers to get his mother out of the room, so that I could spend a few seconds alone with him.

The end result of Adam's continuing sickness and diarrhoea was dehydration. Mr Jackman felt this had to be tackled with transfusions of blood and glucose. But they were impossible to administer and monitor while Adam stayed in isolation.

The crunch had come.

To be certain the bone-marrow transplant had worked and to allow Adam's own system to build up, Mr Kimoto would have preferred to keep Adam in sterile conditions for at least another fortnight. But to do that meant ignoring the serious secondary complications. Now, either they left Adam in isolation, watching him grow worse or they risked letting him out. They just had to hope his immune system was getting strong enough and that they could successfully treat the complications.

I was visiting Adam the evening Mr Jackman put the alternatives to Mrs Simmonds and, instead of taking control, to her enormous credit, she turned straight to Adam. 'You're the only one who can take that decision.'

The impish gleam in Adam's eyes seemed to have faded and his hair hung lank on his forehead. 'I don't see I've got much option, do you?' But I was very relieved when, glancing at me, he added, firmly, 'You will *both* be here for

144

my Coming Out Party, won't you?'

By the following evening, his entire isolation room, already as hygienic as an operating theatre, had been given another thorough scrub-down, in readiness for this momentous occasion.

Before being allowed in, Mrs Simmonds and I were sent into a bathroom to shower, using disinfectant soap to wash away the slightest possibility of our taking in any infection. Mrs Simmonds scrubbed herself so violently with a nail brush, her skin was almost raw. I couldn't help feeling we were behaving like Pontius Pilate and Lady MacBeth, both determined to wash away all traces of our guilt. Ashamed of being so disgustingly healthy compared to Adam. Eventually, squeaky clean and swathed from head to toe in sterile white clothing, like a pair of novice nuns prepared for a ceremony, we were allowed to enter.

Mr Jackman, similarly dressed, was waiting to officiate. 'Ready?' he asked.

We all solemnly nodded.

I held my breath as Mr Jackman tore off the adhesive tape which sealed two sheets of the plastic together. Mrs Simmonds flinched at the harsh noise.

But when the sheets gaped open, nobody moved, not even Adam.

He sat on the edge of his bed, showing no inclination to leave his prison. It was the first time I'd ever seen Adam so unsure of himself. This was a complete reversal of the main rule he'd lived by all his life. In view of all the warnings he'd had, of the fatal consequences of the slightest hole being made in the plastic skin, his hesitation was not so surprising. Now that it was finally punctured, his life-sentence over, Adam looked as if he'd never dare take the first step towards freedom. If Mr Jackman hadn't offered Adam his hand, he might never have moved. Cautiously, Adam took it and was almost pulled towards us. Mr

Jackman was smiling broadly as he handed Adam over to his mother, who enveloped him in their first huge hug.

In spite of everything I'd felt before, I couldn't resent their shared moment – a mother, hugging her sixteen-year-old son for the very first time, with tears streaming down her face into her mask.

As I watched, I knew the time was drawing closer when Adam and I would touch for the first time and I understood how Adam had felt about coming out. It seemed such a mega-step to take. Whilst I'd dreamed of it, never, in my wildest imaginings, had I ever truly believed that this moment would happen.

What did happen wasn't likely to become an entry in *The Guinness Book of Greatest Romantic Moments*!

Having gently extricated himself from his mother's embrace, Adam moved slowly towards me, but either nerves, or the fumbling clumsiness of my gloved hands, must have made me jumpy. We'd barely touched before Adam leapt back as if jolted by an electric shock, except he was giggling, 'Hey! Stop that, it tickles!'

After suffering years of solitary confinement, Adam quickly made up for lost time and soon thoroughly enjoyed the idea of being touched, often rubbing himself against us like a cat. Though heaven knows, the only flesh his visitors were allowed to expose, like women in purdah, was around our eyes.

My main impression of that first day was shock, as Adam suddenly jerked into sharp focus. The fuzzy image I'd got used to, through the intervening plastic, was instantly replaced by a crystal-clear one. The difference was as startling as the change in picture quality when a cranky, old TV is replaced by the latest hi-tech model.

Adam's eyes, which I'd always seen as impish pools of blue-black, now, despite his illness, darted about with all the wicked curiosity of a Siamese cat and his shell-pink lips

146

had developed such sharply defined, almost cutting, edges.

I admit I was totally overwhelmed by being able to be so physically close to Adam. My knees went weak and my stomach tied itself in knots.

Later, I found I was constantly having to resist the temptation to examine him in detail, bit by bit; picking him over, the way monkeys groom their mates for fleas!

Adam was obviously experiencing similar reactions, though he expressed them in a far more positive way. I'll never forget one stolen moment, while Mrs Simmonds was away talking to Mr Jackman.

Adam stood very close and, without taking his eyes off mine, over my robe, his bare hands slowly caressed the outline of my body. Every part of me was explored with meticulous care, as if committing a complete map of me to memory, and all done with the tenderness of a blind person's fingers reading Braille.

Trying not to pass out from pure ecstasy, I apologised as he approached the vast expanses of the Northern Plateau, 'Sorry, breasts haven't arrived yet. A temporary delay in the workshop, I hope!'

'You're perfect the way you are,' he whispered in my ear.

'Sure you wouldn't you like me better with boobs?' I asked breathlessly.

'I can wait,' he said. 'The only thing I wish is, you'd change your perfume.'

Pretending to be hurt, I pulled away. 'You don't like Dettol No. 5?'

'It's growing on me,' he admitted.

'You make it sound like mould!'

'If *you* were mould,' he said, with an idiotic grin, 'I'd want to be the cheese you grew on.'

'You always say the sweetest things!'

'Don't I just!' he admitted with a sigh, before he folded me deep into his arms.

. . .

Days later, as his fever grew worse, Adam first vomited blood. This soon became a regular occurrence. Rapidly, far from being dehydrated, fluid built up in his body, placing particular strain on the heart and lungs.

'Look at me,' he said, waving about the scores of tubes which entered and left his body, 'I'm an octopus!'

But his face was drawn, the skin putty-coloured with dark patches under each eye. There was no doubt he was getting weaker and he knew it.

One evening while we were all gathered round his bed, Adam suddenly voiced the private thoughts of us all. 'This isn't going to work, is it?'

Mr Jackman looked at Mr Kimoto and then sat on the edge of Adam's bed. 'No,' he said, quietly taking Adam's hand and cradling it in his, 'in all honesty, we have to admit it isn't. I'm afraid your body's started rejecting almost everything we give it.'

I couldn't believe what I was hearing. In that moment, all the plans and promises became meaningless. My world was thrown upside down and the future stretched out as nothing more than a vast, dark, interminable space.

I couldn't begin to understand how they could discuss it so calmly, as if Adam was of no more value than an old car Tony had failed to repair.

I looked across to Mrs Simmonds. She'd backed away into a corner of the room and was sobbing uncontrollably to herself, not bothering to wipe away the tears, a crumpled, defeated heap.

Adam seemed the only one who was unmoved. 'Was it the bone-marrow that did this to me?'

Mr Kimoto shook his head. 'Not in itself. I'm positive all traces of impurity were removed before it was introduced into your blood stream. But, for some reason, the experience has placed an unreasonable strain on the rest of your body.'

'And although we've tried all we know,' Mr Jackman said, 'we haven't been able to neutralise any of those problems.'

Hardly trusting myself to speak, I whispered, 'What happens now?'

Neither of the doctors looked at me, or even appeared to have heard the question. It was Adam who spoke. 'Do I have months, or weeks?'

How could he talk about this as if he was planning a holiday?

'More like days,' Mr Jackman said.

Adam took a very deep breath before saying, almost as if he hadn't heard the specialists' verdict, 'Right, then I think for starters, I'd feel more comfortable if we could get rid of all this useless plumbing.' He tugged at the maze of pipes which surrounded him.

Mr Jackman thought for a moment before he replied, 'I admit they don't appear to be achieving anything, so we'll do that straight away, if you're sure?'

'I'm sure,' Adam said.

'Anything else?'

'Can you find my mother a bed somewhere?'

'But I can't leave you here alone!' Mrs Simmonds protested.

Mr Jackman, realising how easily Mrs Simmonds' torrent of emotion could upset Adam, who was being so brave and matter-of-fact, quickly intervened. 'Mrs Simmonds,' he pointed out, 'if you don't get some sleep, you're going to make yourself ill. We have a room down the corridor you can use and I'll give you a sedative so that you get a proper rest.'

'But what if anything . . .' Mrs Simmonds couldn't bring herself to finish the sentence.

Mr Jackman helped out. 'If anything should happen, at least you'll be close by and we can easily come and get you.'

After she'd kissed Adam goodnight, Mr Jackman and Mr Kimoto escorted her from the room.

Left alone with Adam, I had no idea what I could say that wouldn't upset him and get me banished too.

But Adam was in total control. He patted the bed beside him. 'Anne, please come and sit close to me.'

With feet of lead, I slowly crossed the room, knowing the closer I got, the more likely I was to betray my real feelings.

But I needn't have worried, Adam knew exactly what he was doing. Carefully, now the whole point of protecting him from germs had gone, he untied my mask and our lips met in our first, proper kiss. All our rehearsals weren't wasted, but compared to the real thing, they faded into total insignificance.

It was a long, deep kiss, which stirred the depths of my soul, but it still couldn't wipe out the realisation that there were so few to come. Tears welled up and stabbed the insides of my eyelids. I brushed them away quickly as we parted, ashamed at giving in to my negative emotions. 'I'm sorry,' I said and stopped short. 'I don't know what else to say.'

'Don't try, there's nothing to say. We know all there is to know. All the stuff about what we've done, or might do, doesn't mean much any more. It'll only lead to regrets and I don't want you to have any of those. I haven't. Meeting you has been the best thing that's ever happened to me.'

'Oh, Adam,' I said, running my hands through his hair.

'You've taught me so much,' Adam said, thoughtfully, 'not to mention all the things I couldn't experience which you explained to me.' His arm tightened around my waist as he said dreamily, 'There's only one other thing, now that we're properly together, which I could have possibly wished for . . .'

Adam was about to put his wish into words, not that he really needed to, when Mr Jackman returned. He had also removed his mask and was wearing surgical gloves. 'Anne, if you could leave us now, I'd like to sort out Adam's tubes.'

Mr Jackman, knowing how reluctant I usually was to leave Adam, must have been surprised when I raised no objection. 'Okay,' I said, casually kissing Adam, 'see you.'

Mum only had to see my face, when I got home, to know Adam was far worse. 'What's happened?'

I answered in the simplest, baldest terms. 'Adam's going to die.'

Like swearing the instant you leave the head teacher's office after a serious telling-off, there was an enormous sense of relief in having finally used the dreaded D-word. One which had been so tactfully avoided while we were still in Adam's room at the hospital.

Mum hugged me. 'You can't be certain. There's always hope.'

I shook my head. If Adam could accept the facts, I had no choice. 'Not when two of the world's greatest experts on SCID tell you there's nothing they can do.'

Her arms tightened round me. 'Anne, I'm so sorry.'

'Please, don't say any more, Mum, otherwise I'll start to cry and if I start now, I'll never stop.'

'There's nothing wrong with crying.'

'But this isn't the time,' I said, gently removing her arms. 'I have to stay strong for Adam's sake. There are things still to be done. There'll be plenty of time for crying later.'

Mum didn't look so sure, but she was kind enough not to argue. 'Is there anything I can do for you?'

I shook my head. 'I'll just have a bath and an early night.'

She kissed me. 'If there's anything you need, call me.'

I soaked for a long time in a solution of fifty per cent bath-oil before I dried off and used my mother's favourite talc.

At gone eleven, I dressed in sweater and jeans, stuffed some sheets of paper in my pocket, put on a quilted jacket and left the house. I was positive Mum saw, or at least heard me leaving, but she did nothing to stop me.

It was about midnight and apart from a couple of ambulances, their back doors gaping open outside Casualty, the sodium-lit forecourt of the hospital was deserted. Even so, the last thing I wanted was to be stopped, or accidentally bump into somebody who would recognise me. I'd no idea when Mr Jackman normally left. Lately he'd given the impression he was living in the place.

Fortunately, in the evenings, a man replaced Spiderwoman on Reception, but I wasn't taking any chances. I lurked in the doorway, until he was busy talking to a porter, before I set out across the acres of tiled floor and, carefully going behind the Christmas tree, headed for the Ladies.

My footsteps sounded so loud! I was convinced I'd attract somebody's attention. I kept expecting someone to shout out after me, but nobody did.

Once inside, thinking I stood less chance of being stopped if I no longer looked as if I'd just arrived from outside, I slipped off my outdoor coat and hung it on a hook.

I waited a few moments, then, clutching the papers, which I'd brought, to help make me look as if I belonged and was busy going about hospital business, I dodged back into Reception and walked briskly through the double doors leading to the main corridor. Although I met the occasional orderly, nobody challenged me.

I was actually on Adam's corridor, when a voice nearly converted me into a candidate for Intensive Care by calling out, 'Excuse me!'

Not knowing whether to stay or run, I spun round. 'Yes?'

The voice belonged to a worried-looking, little, old man, who was about to lose the trousers of his oversized, blue and white striped pyjamas. 'Please, I can't find the nurse, but I desperately need a lavatory!'

Having successfully got so far, it would be stupid to get caught hanging around the one area where my face was most familiar. If Mrs Simmonds appeared, or Mr Kimoto, everything would be ruined and there might never be another chance.

I had to get rid of the man. Feeling guilty, but with as much authority as I could manage I said, 'Down to the far end of the corridor and to your left,' and then, as he scuttled off, urgently clutching his pyjamas, I muttered under my breath, 'I only hope you find one in time!'

A moment later I was through the outer door of the isolation room and in the lobby.

I peered through the little window, but the only person I could see by the dimmed bedsight light, was Adam, fast asleep.

Very quietly, I let myself in. Apart from his breathing, there was no other sound. The air-pump had long been switched off and now all his pipes and tubes removed too, just as he'd asked.

Lying there asleep, his rumpled hair on the pillow, Adam suddenly looked so small and helpless. There was no time to lose. Any moment a nurse might come to check up on him. Switching off the light, I quickly undressed.

Adam stirred as I lifted the covers and eased in beside him.

'Adam,' I whispered, 'it's Anne.'

His arm reached out and found me, as he asked sleepily, 'What are you doing?'

'I'm here to grant your wish,' I said, kissing him.

'I guessed you knew what I was talking about, but I never really believed you'd think of a way of making it happen.

153

Oh, Anne,' he murmured, 'I do love you so much.'

'I love you far more,' were my last words that night.

Two days later, the weekend before Christmas, Adam died.

While the rest of the world was tearing around, wholly preoccupied with last-minute shopping, parties and final preparations for the festivities, very slowly and without fuss, Death took Adam. Very slowly, he slid away from us and being Adam, to hide any moments of pain, he deliberately kept us busy by finding all kinds of trivial errands.

The whole atmosphere was so unreal, I sometimes felt like a girl out of a fairy tale, sent out on missions of apparently meaningless and impossible tasks, in order to rescue her prince from a terrible fate and thereby win his hand. The only difference was, I'd already won my prince, but nobody would ever be able to rescue him.

Once, as his face creased with pain, he sent me off to fetch his first Coke. Similarly, Mrs Simmonds was despatched to the flower-stall in Reception to bring him freesias, so that he could smell their distinctive perfume.

That was the way Adam tried to keep us, if not happy, at least occupied, thinking about tangible things.

There was no longer room for anything as juvenile as being jealous of Mrs Simmonds. We each had our own separate bond with Adam, each our own pain. Our sole, joint concern was for Adam.

The final moment slipped by almost unnoticed. By late Sunday evening, all three of us were exhausted by the watching and waiting, frantically hoping for the least sign of improvement, but finding none.

Mrs Simmonds and I sat either side of Adam's bed, dozing in our chairs, each holding one of his hands. Outside in the corridor, alone with his grief, sat Mr

Simmonds, who had frequently visited Adam but could only bring himself to spend seconds with him without breaking down.

Suddenly Adam stirred and then whispered, 'I love you.'

'We love you too,' replied Mrs Simmonds.

But Adam's eyes were closed, his struggle for breath had ended and already I could feel his palm growing colder against mine.

16

In years to come, if the memory of Adam's death ever begins to fade, it'll only take the first appearance of Christmas cards in the shops, usually around early September, to bring everything flooding back.

Not that he had the choice, but if Adam had to die, I wish he could have done it at almost any other time of year. Life might have been much easier if he'd chosen some obscure day, like the celebration of the Ultimate Mistake of Judd the Careless, rather than during an anniversary with a four-month run-up, which continues for Twelve Days after the event.

Adam's funeral was hastily sandwiched between the festivities of Christmas and New Year. It was on the only day the vicar happened to be free. It was like coming directly from sun to shade while everything was put on hold.

'It's going to seem odd wearing my black dress for the funeral,' Mel said. 'I've been going to parties in it, but it's the only suitable thing I've got.'

I hadn't been to any parties. Mum and Mel were the only people I'd seen since Adam died. They'd been very good and patient with me, not forcing me to talk but were there if I needed them. 'I shouldn't think Adam would mind. I don't suppose he'd care if you turned up in a multicoloured ski suit, I just wish I didn't have to go.'

'But, Anne, you've got to be there. It's a way of saying goodbye.'

'But I've already done that.'

'You ought to go, even if it's only for Mrs Simmonds' sake.'

She was somebody else I'd avoided, even though we had more in common than anyone, too much in fact and I hadn't felt I could face meeting her yet.

I'd expected to cry a lot, but somehow I just didn't, not at all. I think that really worried Mum. 'There's no harm in letting your feelings out,' she said.

But there was nothing there to come out. Just an awful numbness, a vacuum which nothing and nobody could fill; a socket from which a tooth had been taken. Although you know it can never be replaced, you constantly go back, searching, expecting to find it still there.

That was how it was. Whenever the phone rang, for a microsecond I believed again that it would be Adam. Thoughts I wanted to share with him continually popped into my mind, only to be banished after I realised that was impossible.

But how could somebody whose image remained so clear, whose silky, warm skin I could still feel, simply no longer exist?

Then there were the dreams. Not that I slept much but whenever I did, Adam would be waiting for me. No longer ill, he was never in the hospital, or even in the plastic tent at home, but always free. Usually we were out in the country, somewhere we'd never been together in life. I'd be following a path through a wood or across fields and I'd turn a corner to find Adam sitting, waiting, on a log or a wooden stile. Neither of us spoke in any of the dreams. We just walked together hand in hand, but then his strides began to get longer and longer, until I was left miles behind. Frantically, I tried to catch him up, but I never managed it and when I rounded the next corner, Adam had gone and I woke in a cold sweat.

* * *

The day of the funeral was cold and grey. Mum and I arrived at the same time as the hearse. A strong, bitter wind was sending scurries of dead leaves rattling across the churchyard.

We nodded to Mrs Simmonds, who was sheltering just inside the doorway. I couldn't help noticing how old she suddenly looked. Years, not days, could have passed since I last saw her. Slightly behind her, fading into the stonework, her husband seemed to have lost so much weight since his suit was originally made. It was more difficult than ever to picture him as the sportsman he'd once been.

The church itself was less than a quarter full and most of them were Adam's relatives. It was the school holidays, so, apart from Mel, none of my classmates turned up though Miss Weinstock did, looking surprisingly elegant in a well-tailored, black trouser suit, accompanied by her social worker friend who must have been told.

This didn't seem the moment to break the news that I'd finally abandoned my project on SCID, though I suspect she'd already guessed.

Tony came with Mel, which I thought was really nice of him. Mel had bought a black hat with a matching veil and combined with her little (very little!) black dress, looked exactly like a young Sophia Loren with goose pimples. Beside her, my black reefer jacket and black jeans felt very ordinary.

Behind the Simmonds sat Mr Jackman and Mr Kimoto. I thought they had a nerve to turn up like that. I blamed them for what had happened. After all, without them there wouldn't have been a funeral. I was convinced that if they hadn't persuaded Adam to take part in their experiments, he'd still be alive.

Not having many close relations, unless you count Uncle Graham, I'd never been to a funeral before. It seemed a little like suddenly finding yourself sitting in a stationary car, on the motorway, after the traffic's been brought to a halt by a serious accident.

All the bustle and noise stops and you find yourself surrounded by this group of ill-assorted people, most of whom you've never met before, only separated from each other by a partially transparent, protective shell. Most people try to avoid catching each other's eyes and those with young kids hope they won't do anything too embarrassing before they leave.

Everyone knows they're only there at all because something dreadful has happened and they're all pretending they're not thanking God that, this time at least, it hadn't happened to them. Though you can't escape the uncomfortable reminder that what has occurred means we've all just moved one place nearer the front of the queue.

The first hymn was so unfamiliar that most of us could only half-heartedly join in and our voices were easily drowned by the organ. I couldn't take my eyes off the coffin which stood in front of the altar.

I couldn't believe that Adam was really in there. Poor Adam who, above all people, should have been a free spirit, able to explore the world, had been forced to spend his life as a prisoner. It seemed too cruel that he should end up now, cramped, in that tiny box. It looked so drab without any flowers. Mrs Simmonds had insisted that money should be given to medical research instead.

I was beginning to seriously wish I'd followed my instincts and stayed at home by the time the vicar started to speak. I'd hardly noticed him until that moment. He was a short, stocky, young man with close-cropped blond hair, glittering blue eyes and a very healthy complexion, which seemed rather tactless of him at a funeral.

There was nothing hushed about his energetic voice

either, which fairly bounced off the walls, echoing around the lofty corners of the church. 'We are here today to mourn the passing and celebrate the short life of Adam Simmonds. And it's on occasions such as this, because his life was so short, that I often find myself protesting, why?'

This wasn't the sticking plaster of a few half-truths I'd been expecting and I sat up.

'I wasn't lucky enough to have known Adam, but I've been talking to people who did and afterwards, the one question which struck me was, in the circumstances, how could Adam have had such a full life?'

The vicar gently laid a hand on the polished coffin lid.

'Adam suffered from a disease which, apart from his last few days, isolated him from the world and all those he loved. Because of that alone, he would have been justified in constantly complaining, feeling sorry for himself, even hiding himself away, but he did none of those things. That wasn't Adam's way. He took a more positive view. He always looked forward to the day when he might step out into the world and even though he had no idea when that moment would come, he prepared himself for it as best he could. His mind was constantly active. He read a great deal and, with more excuse than most of us, watched hours of television. Those were his windows he used to look out on to a world he could only dream of entering one day.'

Even now I could not cry, though Mum's hand squeezed mine as if I had.

'Now we must ask what Adam gave us. Apart from his collections of amazingly obscure facts and truly dreadful jokes, above all, Adam gave us a deeper understanding of loving and patience. In my heart I know that Adam has at last achieved the freedom he desired, though sadly for us, it was a freedom which proved impossible to enjoy with us on earth, but we are the losers, not Adam.'

. . .

160

Nobody lingered long at the graveside. As we left the church, a squall of stinging, horizontal rain, driven by the high wind, lashed our faces and as the coffin was lowered I felt I was witnessing a burial at sea.

As I moved away, Mrs Simmonds laid a hand on my arm. 'You must come round soon,' she said, 'I have something Adam left for you.'

'Thanks,' I said, but I had no intention of going. What comfort would I get now from some trinket that Adam had once touched? Instead, like everyone else, I left with my memories of Adam and, in spite of the vicar's words, a feeling of bitterness and anger that Adam had been taken away from me.

Throughout the rest of the holiday, Mum and Mel both came to sit with me from time to time, but I had nothing to say to them and I refused Mel's invitation to join her and Tony to see in the New Year.

The decorations coming down everywhere helped, though even then I refused to let Adam's balloon go and it still bobbed forlornly around my bedroom ceiling.

It was the afternoon of the last day of the Christmas holidays before I finally managed to steel myself to visit Mrs Simmonds.

I'd prepared myself for the almost unbearable idea of returning to a house full of memories and logically I knew Adam would not be there, but I still suffered several serious jolts.

The first caught me completely unawares, though if I'd stopped to think it should have been obvious.

Without a word, Mrs Simmonds showed me into the sitting room, which I'd always thought of as being very cramped, but it had suddenly been transformed into a vast, open space.

Adam's plastic home had gone!

All that remained was a ghostly image, like those mysterious corn-circles; faint grooves in the carpet's pile, left by the weight of the supporting struts. In time, once those were hoovered away, there would be no sign of his existence.

Perhaps, merely because it was so empty, the room had an unused feel about it, almost as if the chairs should be covered. There was a thick layer of dust over all the polished surfaces.

The second severe shock was that Adam's portrait still hung on the wall. Mum's prediction was right. That wasn't the Adam I'd last seen and I desperately tried to avoid his eyes, which seemed to be burning into me.

Without wishing to offend Mrs Simmonds, I knew I had to get out of range of those eyes! 'Would you mind if we sat in the kitchen?'

Although she looked a little surprised, Mrs Simmonds didn't say anything, just shrugged and led the way asking, with no real interest, 'Do you want a cup of tea, or anything?'

Relieved at being able to put off the moment when we would have to say something meaningful to each other, I nodded. 'Please.'

While she put the kettle on I had a chance to look around and was surprised by the mess. She'd always been so tidy and organised, but now dirty dishes were stacked on the draining-board and cupboard doors gaped open. Washed clothes waited to be unloaded from the washing-machine, while dirty laundry was piled high on top. The lid of the pedal-bin was forced upright by the amount of rubbish which spilled over on to the grubby tiled floor.

Not that I'm obsessed with cleanliness, but even our kitchen never got into that state, so I automatically knelt down and started to tidy the rubbish back into the bin.

Mrs Simmonds couldn't have looked more baffled if I'd begun a brass rubbing. 'What are you doing?'

'I thought I'd empty this outside for you,' I said.

She still looked puzzled. 'Oh, if you like.'

When I returned Mrs Simmonds was sitting at the table, which was littered with uncapped sauce bottles, unopened letters, stray cutlery and a hair-drier, gazing into space.

She'd made the tea, but forgotten the milk.

The half-empty milk bottle in the fridge sported a cap of green mould. Apart from that, the fridge was mostly empty. Just several dishes containing unidentifiable leftovers.

What on earth were they eating?

Shocked to find somebody in a worse state than me, I remembered passing the milk on the front doorstep and went to collect it.

'Sixteen years,' she said, as I poured fresh milk into our mugs of tea.

'Sorry?'

She didn't seem to hear me, but kept on talking. 'For sixteen years I've known exactly what had to be done every minute of the day. Routine, that was the secret. If you didn't have a routine, there was no way to get through everything. That's all gone now.'

I was beginning to see what had happened to her. I wished I hadn't been so selfish and that, in spite of my own feelings, I'd come sooner. Gently I suggested, 'There's still Mr Simmonds.'

She gave me a pitying look. 'Oh, he can fend for himself, he doesn't *need* me. Not the way Adam did. Adam depended on me for everything, right down to the last detail.'

'Yes, I know.'

She swung round and glared at me. 'What can you know? I know you two thought you were in love, but you'll meet someone else. You're only young, you've got your whole life

163

ahead of you, but me, I'm too old to start again and have more children, even if I dared after what's happened to Adam.'

She let out a long sigh and collapsed, staring into her tea. 'All those years of worrying about Adam, looking after him. Years of waking in the night, wondering if that noise I could hear was really the air pump, or not, and what is there to show for it all now?'

Mrs Simmonds got up and began to wander round the kitchen, talking to the walls as much as to me. 'Now it's all over, all I want to do is rest. I'm so tired, but still I can't sleep. You see, the place is so quiet. Once Ron's gone to work there's nobody here but me. It was all right while he was off work for the holidays. Even if we didn't speak, at least there was somebody moving about the place, somebody to talk to. There's nobody now.'

'I tell you what, why don't you go and have a lie down now, while I'm here?'

'I couldn't do that, not in the middle of the afternoon.'

'Of course you can. Just half an hour and I'll wake you with a cup of tea.'

'Well, all right, but I won't sleep,' she protested.

She did though. I spent over an hour cleaning out the fridge, washing the dirty dishes and generally tidying things up a bit.

I'd scrubbed the kitchen floor before I made her the promised cup of tea, but when I took it through, Mrs Simmonds was still fast asleep and for the first time I saw her looking quiet and peaceful.

17

I created my own file marked Pending and crawled into it, but whatever happens in our own lives, the one thing we can be certain of is, the rest of the world carries on regardless.

Outside school, apart from Mum and Mel, the only other person I saw was Mrs Simmonds.

For some time, she also remained in a state of limbo and I was able to be useful. We rarely mentioned Adam and most of my visits were spent doing practical things, like helping to catch up with the housework. I occasionally even cooked meals for them both.

During those weeks I only went home to sleep, but I was getting comfort from knowing we shared an identical problem and also some satisfaction from being able to help, in a practical way, somebody worse off than me.

Slowly Mrs Simmonds recovered and took up the reins of her own life again and I found myself redundant. I still visited, but she no longer really needed me and once again I went into a state of suspended animation.

Somehow I managed to keep up with school work, which wasn't easy, especially as I had to start and complete a new project from scratch. Miss Weinstock suggested teaming up with Andrew and I really wasn't keen at first. Most people at school didn't know how to talk to me any more and kept as far away as possible. Just the fact that he was a boy I found difficult to deal with, but he turned out to be quite understanding. Very patient and not a bit pushy. He'd even got quite a decent sense of humour, not as black as Adam's, but okay.

Mel's new project was on the history of the internal combustion engine and Miss Weinstock complained she didn't understand most of it!

But throughout it all, I continued to feel as if I was walking around all the time staring at the pavement and so, when I next looked up, I was amazed to find it was suddenly spring and there were daffodils dancing on the Simmonds' back lawn, where Adam had once done his gorilla impression.

Mel had been going out exclusively with Tony for over four months!

'I can't believe it either,' Mel admitted, adding as she dug deep into the pot of Mucky Paws, essential for when she arrived smothered in oil after delving into another of Tony's engines. 'Besides which,' she wailed, 'it's ruining my nails!'

'Don't worry, you'll soon come to your senses.'

She laughed and then suddenly looked quite serious. 'That's what I thought, but now I don't think it's very likely. I'm positive I've found my one true love.'

'Tony?'

Mel smiled. 'And car engines!'

'And just think,' I said proudly, 'it was all thanks to me.'

'True.'

'If I hadn't persuaded Tony to ring you, you'd still be smelling of Chanel instead of Mobil Multi-grade. Though I have to admit, at first, I thought you were just on the rebound from Rob.'

'Rob! That reminds me!' She dried her hands and pulled from her bag a large envelope which she waved around triumphantly.

'What is it?'

'Those sick photographs Rob took of me. Not just the

166

prints but the negatives too!'

'How on earth did you get hold of those?'

'Tony got them back for me. You remember Rob skipped town soon after we broke up? Well, Tony met him in town the other day – met being the operative word! I'm glad that's all over and done with. He's quite a fantastic fella, my Tony. By the way, have I told you, I've definitely decided to go to Engineering College?'

Though thoughts of Adam were never out of my mind, I thought I was beginning to recover, until one day I came home and Mum gave me a message from Mr Jackman, which brought everything flooding back.

It seemed that a little girl, suffering from leukaemia, was desperately in need of a bone-marrow transplant. Without it, she'd almost certainly die. They'd kept my details on file from the tests I'd done for Adam, and I was an identical match. Would I do it?

I really didn't want to go back to that hospital, or meet Mr Jackman again. Ever since Adam's death, Mr Jackman and Mr Kimoto had been the focus of all my anger. I hadn't been able to bring myself to speak to them at the funeral. I know it wasn't logical, but I still blamed them for what had happened to Adam, as surely as if they'd murdered him.

Mr Jackman's call revived all that anger, but when I found out the appointment wasn't to be with him, but with the Head Vampire, I reluctantly decided to go.

The moment I presented myself in Reception, Robot Woman, who's never been good at allowing me to go where I want to, tried to redirect me yet again. 'Mr Jackman's left a message to say he'd like a word with you first.'

'But I don't have an appointment with him,' I smugly pointed out.

'He's waiting for you, now.'

Even as I made my way down the familiar corridor, I could feel myself tensing up with anger.

'You still haven't forgiven us, have you, Anne?' Mr Jackman said the moment I sat down in his office. Mr Kimoto had long since returned to Japan.

'No, I haven't,' I replied. 'If Adam hadn't agreed to your experiment, he might still be alive today. You've no right to try things out on people until you know they're safe.'

'Safe?' Mr Jackman looked surprised. 'Anne, nothing in life is safe. When you leave here, you could walk straight out under a bus.'

'But at least that would be *my* fault, not yours.'

Mr Jackman nodded. 'True, but we gave Adam a choice. He could have stayed "safe", as you call it. But Adam knew, as well as us, that standing still could be every bit as dangerous as moving forwards. Anne, you must understand, there are no certainties with SCID. Mrs Simmonds told you about Sarah, Adam's baby sister?' I nodded. 'Although we tried, we were unable to keep Sarah alive. But, from trying to save her, we learned things, things which helped Adam and others like him. Science isn't always about sudden, miraculous discoveries. Sometimes you move painfully slowly, one step at a time.'

I was sickened. 'And that's all Adam was to you, a step?'

Mr Jackman was dismayed. 'Oh, no, far more. If he was anything, Adam was a giant leap forward. Mainly because he'd survived so much longer than most children born with SCID. He advanced our knowledge enormously. Adam knew the enormity of the risk he was taking, but he believed it was worth it. If not for him, then for the next . . .'

'And the next?' I asked. 'And the next, and the next . . . How many have to die?'

'Only until the first one *doesn't*,' Mr Jackman said. 'You

must remember, Adam isn't the only child to suffer from SCID, there are many others. You must realise, Adam saw our work as a positive contribution he could help us make for others too. If he hadn't, he wouldn't have allowed us to continue, because that's all he had to get him through it all. That and a few loving, understanding people, like you. Which is why I wanted to offer you the opportunity to do something positive now – help this little girl who has leukaemia.'

Remembering Sarah and Adam, how could I refuse?

I'm glad I didn't. The little girl is getting along fine. Although it isn't usual, I was allowed to see her. Her name's Charlotte and she's like a tiny, china doll, with a mass of curly, blonde hair and huge blue eyes. Mr Jackman says she'll be okay now and I'm really pleased for her.

Sometimes, when you least expect it, science moves much faster than one step at a time. A few weeks after I saw Mr Jackman, I read about a new drug that's being developed in this country which could be used to cure SCID. In America doctors are also having some success with taking blood from SCID sufferers, treating it with gene therapy to strengthen their natural resistance to disease, and then returning it to the patient.

I only wish those treatments had been around in time for Adam, though of course nobody knows if they'll work yet, but I hope something does soon.

One thing which has helped me a great deal is that Mum's always around these days when I need her. We don't talk a lot, but the company's good. This has come about because in February she heard she'd won a massive prize in an art competition. She got it for one of the pencil sketches she did of Adam before painting his portrait. The picture was mine really and I said she could enter it on condition it was marked not for sale. Anyway, with the money she won, she's been able to give up work, at least for a while, and concentrate on her painting. Maybe, now she has more time to paint and because of the publicity from winning the prize, she may never have to go back to typing. I certainly hope so, she deserves it.

Oh, and I've got a prize too, a sort of booby prize! Yes, for some mysterious reason, I've finally sprouted breasts. Not in Mel's league, mine are more like tangerines than melons, but at least they're breasts. It seems an awful pity they arrived too late for Adam to admire them, but I'm sure he'd be proud of me.

Yesterday, while I was round at Adam's house, Mrs Simmonds handed me an envelope. 'I was sorting out the bureau the other day and I found this.'

'What is it?'

'It's a letter Adam wrote you after the tubes were out. He gave it to me to look after, with strict instructions to destroy it if he ever recovered. I put it away for safety in a drawer. You remember, I told you at the funeral Adam left something for you? Well, with one thing and another, it kept slipping my mind and I only found it again this morning.'

I'd never bothered to ask her about that because I'd always thought she meant just some silly keepsake that might have nothing to do with Adam.

Resisting the urge to rip open the envelope immediately, I ran home and up into my room.

Just seeing his black, spidery writing, close up for the first time, would have been enough to set my engine racing, but the sensation that this was, almost, a communication from beyond the grave, sent me into overdrive! I'm not sure what I expected the contents to be, but this is what I got:

Dear Anne,

This is a really weird letter to write because if you get to read it, I won't be around any more and I'm sure if this had happened the other way round, and I was the one left behind, I'd be devastated.

But you're much more sensible and besides, I need you to do one more thing for me.

You've always been so brilliant at tasting things, promise me you will put all this behind you and go out now and taste real life!

I'd rather you didn't forget me altogether, but you mustn't let me get in the way. You have to get on with your own life.

I know a few bad things happened to us, but you brought such a change into my life. You are a very special person that all my memories of you are good ones and being us, together that one night, was the best, most brilliant thing that ever happened to me.

I don't want you to have any regrets, I haven't, but now the time has come when *you must let me go*.

Promise?

All of my love for ever,

Adam.

When I looked up from Adam's letter, it was to see the shiny red balloon he'd sent me, the day of the operation, still bobbing around on the ceiling.

Every morning when I woke, there it was grinning at me; the shiny surface magnifying the slightest glimmer of light. I don't ever remember having one that lasted so long. When I was little, ordinary balloons usually burst before I got them home and even the metallic-surfaced, gas-filled ones, like Adam's, always sprang a leak and went wrinkly within days. But not this time. Whenever I went into the room, the slightest breath of air sent it scudding around the ceiling; its printed face grinning down at me.

Somehow though, today the expression on the face seemed to have changed, almost as if it was checking up on me, to see if I've done what Adam said and let him go, and of course I hadn't.

Slowly, I began to realise what he meant. Souvenirs are all very well, but in the end they're all like the stones we pick up off the beach during a particularly special holiday and there has to come a day when that stone no longer means what it used to. It's not as if the stone holds the heat of the day when it was picked up and in a funny kind of way, when it's touched, it no longer even has the same texture it used to have.

It's just become the vague centre for a whole lot of memories; while the person, the boy you met on that beach and who no longer writes, he never was *truly* part of that stone. Admit it, you picked it up while he wasn't even looking! So the stone's become just another paperweight, gathering dust on your desk. And if your being together, you and that boy, meant anything at all, the best parts are in your head, stored away for ever. You're stuck with those, whether you want them or not, but finally you have to let the real boy go, if that's the way things turn out.

I knew, just as he'd said in his letter, the time had come to let Adam go and I knew how it had to be done. Feeling like a big, soft kid, trailing a red balloon behind me, I went to the park.

As this was to be very private, and was going to hurt, I had to get away from all the other people. I walked right up to the top of the steep hill in the centre.

Twice I nearly decided to take the thing home again, but I knew that wasn't an option any more.

Finally, I forced my fingers to release the string and then, as I watched the balloon soaring up into a perfectly clear, blue sky, getting tinier every second, for the first time since Adam died, I cried my eyes out.

Also by Ian Strachan

The Flawed Glass
Shortlisted for the 1989 Whitbread Award

As a true islander Shona has always had a strong belief in
the impossible and in magic. When her uncle leaves for
America the magic seems to fade but Shona cannot stop
praying for the miracle that will unlock what is stored
away in a body that can hardly walk and a tongue that
cannot speak. When an American businessman arrives as
a laird of Shona's remote island off the coast of Scotland
the miracle does happen in the most unexpected way...

'This makes an absorbing read leaving the reader with
much to ponder.'
Books for Keeps

A Selected List of Fiction from Mammoth

While every effort is made to keep prices low, it is sometimes necessary to increase prices at short notice. Mandarin Paperbacks reserves the right to show new retail prices on covers which may differ from those previously advertised in the text or elsewhere.

The prices shown below were correct at the time of going to press.

☐	7497 0978 2	**Trial of Anna Cotman**	Vivien Alcock	£2.50
☐	7497 0712 7	**Under the Enchanter**	Nina Beachcroft	£2.50
☐	7497 0106 4	**Rescuing Gloria**	Gillian Cross	£2.50
☐	7497 0035 1	**The Animals of Farthing Wood**	Colin Dann	£3.50
☐	7497 0613 9	**The Cuckoo Plant**	Adam Ford	£3.50
☐	7497 0443 8	**Fast From the Gate**	Michael Hardcastle	£1.99
☐	7497 0136 6	**I Am David**	Anne Holm	£2.99
☐	7497 0295 8	**First Term**	Mary Hooper	£2.99
☐	7497 0033 5	**Lives of Christopher Chant**	Diana Wynne Jones	£2.99
☐	7497 0601 5	**The Revenge of Samuel Stokes**	Penelope Lively	£2.99
☐	7497 0344 X	**The Haunting**	Margaret Mahy	£2.99
☐	7497 0537 X	**Why The Whales Came**	Michael Morpurgo	£2.99
☐	7497 0831 X	**The Snow Spider**	Jenny Nimmo	£2.99
☐	7497 0992 8	**My Friend Flicka**	Mary O'Hara	£2.99
☐	7497 0525 6	**The Message**	Judith O'Neill	£2.99
☐	7497 0410 1	**Space Demons**	Gillian Rubinstein	£2.50
☐	7497 0151 X	**The Flawed Glass**	Ian Strachan	£2.99

All these books are available at your bookshop or newsagent, or can be ordered direct from the address below. Just tick the titles you want and fill in the form below.

Cash Sales Department, PO Box 5, Rushden, Northants NN10 6YX.
Fax: 0933 410321 : Phone 0933 410511.

Please send cheque, payable to 'Reed Book Services Ltd.', or postal order for purchase price quoted and allow the following for postage and packing:

£1.00 for the first book, 50p for the second; **FREE POSTAGE AND PACKING FOR THREE BOOKS OR MORE PER ORDER.**

NAME (Block letters) ....

ADDRESS..

....

☐ I enclose my remittance for ....

☐ I wish to pay by Access/Visa Card Number ☐☐☐☐☐☐☐☐☐☐☐☐☐☐☐☐

Expiry Date ☐☐☐☐

Signature ....

Please quote our reference: MAND